Buddy

Beware
of
Things
like :

m murphy

The Secrets of Pilgrim Pond

Case No. 4

A Belltown Mystery

By
T. M. Murphy

J. N. TOWNSEND PUBLISHING
EXETER, NEW HAMPSHIRE
2001

Printed in Canada
Published by J. N. Townsend Publishing
    4 Franklin Street
    Exeter, NH 03833
    603/778-9883
    800/333-9883
    www.jntownsendpublishing.com
    www.belltownmysteries.com

I'd like to thank Chris Ryan, Richard Lyons, Ken Gucwa, Susan Saint James, Kathy Mortenson, Jim Miller, Rick Sample, Gerry Callahan, Joanne Byron, Fence, and John Gagnon for all their help during the tough times.

I would like to thank all of the students I have had over the years in the Just Write It Class especially the ones who kept me writing during one long winter: Christine Lindberg, Julia Cox, Ashley & Emily Yoerger, Casey Guerin, Danny Madani, Devin Sibson, Libby Dougherty, Kate Murphy, Teddy Noonan, Karen Truscott, Jonathan Urbach, and Erin Ringland.

For Seton:
There is only one thing better than having a friend—
having a brother who's a friend.

CHAPTER ONE

PSYCHED. ON TOP of the world. That's how I should've felt. Life couldn't get any better for me. Let me tell you why. First off, when I returned from Ireland my mom presented me with a key to our garage. It turns out that while I was away she finished having the two-car garage renovated into a guest room with a woodstove, a bathroom, and a small kitchen. I knew she had some carpenters transforming the garage into a guest house—I just didn't know I was the guest! I was going to have my own space. It was a dream come true. Psyched. On top of the world. That's how I should've felt.

I figured now that I had my own place, which I dubbed The Shack, I could open a detective agency or at least take on some cases. In fact, I had already solved two cases. The first one was when the local supermarket hired me to find out who was stealing their shopping carts; twelve had been stolen in the last month. After a day and night of surveillance, I found the guilty party to be a bag boy named Ethan Norwich. He stole the shopping carts not for the carts but for the wheels. He would take the wheels off and sell them to his friends. They were into soapbox racing and they would use the wheels for the front of their vehicles. The supermarket paid me fifty bucks. Psyched. On top of the world. That's how I should've felt. I know. I know. I keep saying that, but now I'll get to the point of why I didn't feel that way.

I sat at my desk eyeing the gift certificate for a CD at Spinnaker Records Store that Larry Bauer gave me as payment for the case I had just solved for him—The Case of the Forged Love Letters.

Bauer was a freshman who kept getting love letters from Kim Archer, a senior and head cheerleader. He hired me to find out if it was really Kim Archer and not just someone playing a joke. He told me it seemed too good to be true. Well, Larry Bauer was right. It was too good to be true. There was no return address on the envelopes but they were postmarked Baywood not Belltown. Baywood was the town next to Belltown. I asked Larry if he knew anyone from Baywood. He told me his ex-girlfriend lived there—case solved.

It really didn't take Sherlock Holmes to figure out these cases, and that's why I wasn't psyched or on top of the world. I sat with my feet on my desk, staring at the gift certificate, thinking about the past year. With the help of friends, I had uncovered things that were meant for the movies, not real life. But now, I had to accept the fact that not every day was going to be a "Magnum P.I." episode for Orville Jacques.

Life was slowing down for me, and I had to come to terms with that. Maybe all my exciting adventures were over. I really think I was about to accept those terms, that is, until *she* walked into my office.

"Hi ... I'm ... are you ... ah ... Orville Jacques?" A girl with long blonde hair stood in my doorway. I gave a quick nod, threw my gift certificate down, and kicked my feet off the desk. The girl totally caught me off guard.

"Oh, I'm sorry, your mother said to go right in. I thought this was just a garage." She apologized while scanning the place.

"It *was* just a garage but we had it winterized. It's my place now." I got up and walked over to her.

"Wow! How cool. Your own place." The girl was impressed.

"Yeah, well, my parents are pretty cool people."

She looked at me a little bewildered.

"I mean for parents," I added with a nervous laugh. The girl smiled, as I was trying to place her. I had seen her before. But, I knew she didn't go to Belltown High because I definitely would have known who she was. There is no getting around the fact that she was a natural beauty.

"What can I do for you, Miss—?" I tried to act formal.

"Hyde. Vanessa Hyde."

"Why don't I know you? The name sounds so familiar."

"I go to Belltown Academy."

"Oh." That explained it. Snob. All the rich kids went there.

"But, really, I'm not a snob," Vanessa added quickly.

"I didn't say you were." I tried to keep a straight face. She had read my mind.

"You didn't say it, but I know you probably thought that. All the kids who go to Belltown High think that."

"Well, ah..." I was going to argue but the truth was I had no argument.

"No, no"—she put her hand up to stop me—"for the most part they're right. A lot of kids I go to school with are snobs. They make me sick." She apparently wanted to make this point.

"OK. OK. You're not a snob, Vanessa, so what can I do for you?" I helped her off with her winter coat.

"Thank you," she said, and I motioned for her to sit down in the chair across from my desk. She settled in her seat before she answered. "Well, Orville, I've read in the newspaper all about you and the case you solved this past summer."

"Yes." I sat down behind my desk.

"And, I've asked around and heard you're taking on cases now." She stopped. She seemed quite hesitant.

"Yes." I gave her the word so she could continue.

"Well, I was wondering if you would consider taking my case. I would like you to find out something for me."

"What would that be—*Vogue's* spring fashions or who's dating the captain of our hockey team?" I knew immediately that I shouldn't have said that. Vanessa got up from her chair and picked up her coat.

"I'm sorry. I was just kidding." I followed her. She put on her coat.

"Obviously, this was a huge mistake. I heard you were different from other guys. I was told I could come to you for help. I guess Maria was wrong." Vanessa opened the door.

"Maria!" Maria Simpkins was my ex-girlfriend who now lived in Florida.

"Yes, Maria and I took ballet classes together growing up. When I found out you used to date her I called her in Florida. I told her about my problem and she said I should contact you. She said if there is anyone who has the heart to help, it is Orville Jacques."

"She said that?" I was stunned that she still thought of me.

"Don't worry, I won't tell her how far off she was." Vanessa headed out the door.

"Wait, Vanessa. I'm sorry about the joke. I was being stupid. It's just that I've had some pretty lame cases lately. Really, I want to help you. I'm a jerk but not as big a jerk as you might think I am." I smiled and motioned for her to come back and sit down. She didn't move. She was still deciding.

"Vanessa, who else will help you? And you can't beat my rates. A CD for an easy case. Three CDs for a hard one."

Vanessa finally came over and sat down. She gave a half smile.

"Well, if that's how you charge, I'm probably going to owe you a whole record store." She reached into her pocket and pulled out a folded up envelope.

"Even if you decide not to help me, I have to know that you'll keep this meeting secret." Her blue eyes gave me a long stare.

"You have my word." I reached out and took the envelope. The words were typed. I read them out loud.

"Miss Vanessa Hyde, 22 Saltwater Lane, Belltown, MA 02134."

"There is no return address and the postmark is Boston," Vanessa added.

I opened the envelope and pulled out a piece of velvet material that had been cut into a square, and studied it.

"I'm terrible with colors. What color would you say this is?"

"Lavender."

"Lavender," I repeated as I turned it over and saw a small white label attached to it. On the label was an even smaller black X.

"OK." I looked back at her. "You want me to find out who sent you this?" I asked, trying to sound upbeat, but talk about trying to find a needle in a haystack!

"There's more. I can trust you, right, Orville?" Vanessa was still wavering.

"Yes." I was getting anxious.

"This letter was also in the envelope." She placed the letter on the desk.

The words on the paper were in different sizes and shapes. They had been cut out of magazines and glued onto the paper. The letter read:

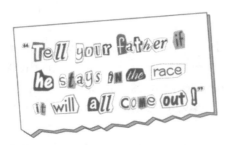

"Race? Wait a second, your last name is Hyde. Of course, your father is Douglas Hyde the guy who's running for Congress." I put it all together. I thought, she's probably thinking what a great detective.

"Yes, that's my father. Can you help me? I have to find out what all of this means." She wasn't holding back her anxiety. It was clear she was afraid.

"Well, did you ask your dad what it means?" I asked the logical question.

"Of course, I did. Father just exploded and said he never wanted to talk about it. He told me to forget it. Can you believe that, Orville? Like I could really forget that I received a death threat on my father's life." Vanessa's eyes were filling up.

"Hold on, now. Don't think that way. Yes, it is a threat, but we don't know if it is on your father's life. What we do know"—I paused and picked up the material and studied it again—"is that we have a piece of lavender-colored velvet material with a small *X* on the label. The *X* could stand for X-tra large which might indicate a size of men's clothing."

"But the color is lavender and the material is velvet. That doesn't sound like men's clothing," Vanessa pointed out.

"I know, but it looks to me like very old material. It might come from a smoking jacket, like the kind they wear in all the old movies. I'll have it checked out." I placed it in the envelope and put the envelope into my desk drawer.

"I just hope my father doesn't notice that it's missing. You see, he took it from me and hid it in his room, but I found it under his pillow."

"You're not close to your father, are you?" I asked.

"No. Not as close as I'd like to be. I love my father but he always has been into his work, even before my mother divorced him. Now, it's just worse. But, how did you know we weren't close?" Vanessa was intrigued.

"You call him Father. That's very formal. You haven't once referred to him as Dad."

"That's interesting how you figured that out. But, I want you to know something. Whether I call him Father or Dad, I do love him and I have to find out the truth about this," she said firmly.

"After I have the material checked out, you'll be the first to know," I assured her.

"How are you going to have it checked out?"

"I have my ways." I knew exactly who to go to.

"Well, thank you, Orville." Vanessa shook my hand and turned toward the door.

"No, problem. But, Vanessa, one thing before you leave."

"Yes?" She turned back.

"You're going to have to be prepared to deal with whatever I find out about your father." I gave her a serious look.

"Yes, I understand. I'll deal with it." Vanessa nodded slowly.

As Vanessa shut the door I realized she had put all of her faith in me to find the truth, and no matter what it was she was going to have to deal with her father's secret. I wondered whatever that secret was, could I discover it? But most of all, could I deal with it and help her!

There is a saying: Be careful what you wish for because you might just get it. I had wished for an exciting case to challenge my senses, and now I had one. Of course, it might turn out to be nothing big, I thought. But, my gut told me it was something huge, and I have learned from experience that I should listen to my instincts and not my head.

It had all happened so quickly that I forgot to ask Vanessa the obvious questions like, Does your father have any enemies? or Who wouldn't want him in Congress? I had to work quickly. A threat means do this *or else*. It was my job to make sure Vanessa and her father didn't find out what the "or else" part meant. I opened my desk drawer and studied the fabric again. All I had was this small piece of material for a clue. But, I tried not to look at the negative aspect. Being negative never got anyone anywhere.

"So what's the positive?" I asked myself out loud.

At least I had a clue, I thought, even if it was a small one. Sometimes, the oddest and most meaningless clues answer the roughest questions. I don't exactly know if that's true but it sounded like a good theory, and I brightened up a bit at the thought of it.

"Where do I begin?" I asked out loud. "You can't find out who the hunter is if you don't know why they're hunting the prey. So you must find out about the prey," I said while rubbing my chin with my index finger.

Where did I hear that one? Too many "Remington Steele" reruns or was it Sherlock Holmes who said that? But whichever one it was, the statement was true. I had to find out everything about the prey. In this case, the prey was candidate for Congress Douglas Hyde.

I jumped out of my chair and went over to the wall phone.

Along with The Shack my mom had also given me my own phone line. I remember thanking her and her saying: "You won't thank me when the phone bills come in. It's your phone. That means *your* bills." I just laughed. I had everything a detective needed except for a computer and that's where Gina Goldman came in. I dialed her number and let it ring. Gina was my best girl friend, and she was a computer genius. She had used her computer once to help me solve a murder mystery that was about fifty years old.

"Yes, hello." Gina picked up after the fifth ring. She was out of breath.

"Gina, it's Orville. Where were you?"

"Practicing my karate."

"Karate? Since when did you start taking karate?" I wasn't sure if she was joking or not.

"About two months ago. I just busted my first two by four with my bare hand!" she said excitedly.

"You're kidding, right?" I wasn't going to fall for it.

"No, really I'm serious. I haven't told anyone because I wasn't sure if I was going to stick with it, but over the holiday break I really got into it." Gina's voice was sincere. This was no joke.

"What made you want to take up karate?" I asked. For a moment I forgot about the case.

"Well, I was watching that old 'wipe on, wipe off movie. Y' know. What's it called?"

"The Karate Kid." I helped her.

"Well, anyway, I really got into the movie, and wham, here I am breaking boards, listening to my disco!"

Gina Goldman was definitely different but that was one reason why I liked her. The other was that I knew I could count on her.

"So what's up, Orville?"

"Well, I need your help." I knew what her response would be.

"Cool. A case, right?"

"Yeah."

"OK, let me get a pen and some paper. Wait a sec."
Finally, Gina got back on.

"This isn't about Larry Bauer getting the love letters from Kim Archer, is it?"

"No, I already figured that one out. They were forged. Ex-girlfriend." That's all I had to say.

"That's what I figured. Larry's a nice kid but he's only a freshman. Anyway, he's better off. Kim Archer is..."

Before she could continue I cut her off. "OK. Have you heard of a guy named Douglas Hyde?"

"Yeah, he's running for Congress."

"Do you know anything else about him?"

Gina wasn't only a disco-listening, karate-kicking, computer genius, she also had an ear out for what was going on in town.

"All I know is his wife left him about four years ago. I think she lives somewhere in Europe or something. He's a scientist. So, he keeps to himself, y'know what I mean. Except for this election, now he has to be a public person. He has a daughter. What's her name?" she thought out loud.

"Vanessa." I let it slip out.

"Oh, is that your client?"

"No." I had to keep that confidential. At least for now, I thought.

"So, what is a scientist doing running for Congress?" I asked quickly.

"He's an environmentalist. He wants to keep Cape

Cod beautiful. Y'know, save it from big business."

Possible motive right there, I thought.

"Orville, haven't you read about him in the paper?"

"If he's not in the box score, I don't know who he is," I confessed.

"Some detective." Gina tried to get me going, but I wasn't going to play along.

"I need you to find out all you can about this Hyde guy on your computer."

"No problem. But, Orville, what's this thing with you and people who are associated with Congress?" Gina laughed. She was referring to a case I had solved involving a retired congressman.

"Let's hope Mr. Hyde is different." I took a deep breath.

"Orville, you're going to have to do two things for me before I risk arrest and break into any systems for you."

I knew there would be a price to pay.

"Tell me what's this all about for one, and two, give me the gift certificate Larry Bauer gave you for a free CD at Spinnaker's." Gina was now all business.

"OK. When you get the information on Hyde come by The Shack and I will fill you in and you'll get the certificate. Just, please don't buy any more disco music," I begged.

"I've had my eye on *The Best of the 70s* for a while now," she roared. She knew this would turn my stomach.

"Gina, before I go. How did you know Larry gave

me a gift certificate for a CD? I didn't tell anyone."

"Orville Jacques, you're not the only sleuth in Belltown, Cape Cod. Later." Gina hung up before I could say anything else.

Vanessa Hyde had hired me to help her. No one else. I felt a little guilty that I was sort of going against her wishes and was going to include Gina. But, Gina could find out things with her computer in minutes that might take me days, and, from the threatening letter, I knew I didn't have days. I put on my coat and grabbed the lavender material and shoved it into my pocket. I had to have this checked out in a lab, I thought. There was only one person I knew who could help me—Shane O'Connell.

CHAPTER
TWO

DETECTIVE SHANE O'CONNELL of the Belltown Police Department sat behind his desk with his hands folded behind his head. He stared into my eyes. I knew exactly what the staring was for. He told me once he could read people by looking into their eyes. He was reading me.

"Orville, don't even ask." Shane sat up.

"What ever happened to 'Hi, Orville. It's good to see you. How was your trip to Ireland?'" I put my hand out. Shane reluctantly got up and shook it.

"So, you just stopped by to tell me you're back in town and you just wanted to say hi." His voice had an air of suspicion to it.

"Well, you know you've become a good buddy to me this past year..."

Shane interrupted, "Shut the door and get to the

point, Orville. I know you're here for something. What is it?"

Shane was serious, and I felt a little uneasy, so I decided not to joke around, to just come to the point.

After I shut the door, he broke out into a full smile.

"Scared you, didn't I?" He laughed.

"I wouldn't say you scared me but it certainly wasn't the warmest reception." I was relieved. I thought he was mad at me.

"It's just that I'm onto you, Orville. I heard you're taking cases now. So you must want something."

"OK. You're right." I handed him the piece of lavender material.

"What's this?" He studied it.

"I was kind of hoping you could tell me. Are you still friends with that guy who works for the FBI?" I was expecting him to give me some lecture about how you can't go to the FBI over something trivial. Instead, Shane burst into laughter.

"Orville Jacques, you are something else!"

"What?" I had no clue as to what he was laughing about.

"You knew I was going to Boston tomorrow to have lunch with Mel. Didn't you?"

"Well." I smiled and shrugged my shoulders. I was going to play along. It was a coincidence but I wasn't going to tell Shane. What he didn't know wouldn't hurt him.

"How did you find that out? Did Officer Jameson tell you?" He went over and poured two cups of coffee.

"Let's just say I have my ways." I laughed.

"Cream?" Shane asked.

"Yup and four sugars," I added.

"How can you taste the coffee?" He shook his head.

"That's the point, I can't." He handed me the mug and I took a sip.

"So, Shane, do you think you could ask your friend Mel to have this material checked out in the FBI lab? It's really important I find out what this material is from and soon."

"Well, what's this case you took, anyway?" Shane rubbed his mustache.

"You know I can't tell you that. I have an obligation to my client to keep things secret." I took another sip.

"So, the first place you come to is the police station," Shane said with a slight edge to his voice.

"Hey, that's a low blow. I thought you might be able to help me. But, if you don't want to..."

"Slow down there, Orville. You know I have to make you beg a little." Shane got serious, "I still owe you my life."

"Well, you did pay me back for that." I didn't want him to think I forgot how he saved my life.

"Yeah, well that was nothing." Shane seemed to be a little embarrassed.

"Mel does owe me a few favors. I suppose I could have him check this out."

"Awesome. Thanks, Shane!"

"Hold on."

Here it comes, I thought.

"You must think this will be something big, right. I mean this isn't some little case is it?"

"To be honest with you, I don't know. My gut tells me it's something big," I confessed.

"I've learned to trust your crazy instincts. So if this does turn out to be something the police should know about, you better come to me—or else." He gave me a stern look.

"Yes, or else." I nodded but drifted into thinking about the threatening letter to Vanessa Hyde. What did "it will all come out" mean? I had to find out and soon. My friend Shane O'Connell would help me try to overcome my first obstacle: finding out what the lavender material was. But, I knew if I overcame that obstacle, it would just be the beginning. The beginning of what? was the question that ran through my mind as I walked out of the Belltown Police Department.

When I returned from the police department, I found a folder in The Shack with a note attached.

I have karate class tonight so I couldn't wait around. Here's all the stuff I could find out about Douglas Hyde. Not very interesting. I'll pick you up for school at 7:00 and you better tell me what this is all about! Peace, G.

I placed the folder on my desk and then went over to the woodstove and put two logs in to bring the fire back to life. I wondered for a second how Gina got into my place since she didn't have a key and there were no signs of forced entry. Then, I realized Gina was capable of doing anything, so why waste time thinking about that when there was a more pressing matter: Douglas Hyde. Once I was comfortable in my chair, I opened the folder and scanned the personal bio Gina put together in her own words.

Name: Douglas Hyde

Age: 43

Marital Status: Divorced

Children: Elizabeth Hyde: deceased. (Orville, she drowned when she was eight.)

Vanessa Hyde: National Honor Society, Field Hockey Captain, Figure Skating Club, President of Science Club.

Hmmm, I thought, she's into science just like her father.

I returned to some newspaper articles Gina had also included. The articles focused on Douglas Hyde running for Congress because he wanted to keep Cape Cod a tourist attraction for "all the good reasons—nature, environment."

It went on to say: "I have lived in Belltown, Cape Cod, all my life and I know the people do not want big business to ruin our beaches, our ponds, our forests, and most of all, our way of life."

I couldn't have agreed more with the man as I read on about different issues he stood for, but Gina was right, it was boring. It went on and on about how he supported the closing of Fisherman's Banks to fishing for six years so the fish population could replenish, etc.

I hadn't learned anything really new except that he worked at the Belltown Oceanographic, and he had a daughter who drowned. I had to find out more about the man, himself, and not his issues. Luckily, Dr. Wilder, a good friend of our family, worked at the Belltown Oceanographic. I could pick his brain and find out what kind of person Douglas Hyde was.

I put another log on the fire and reluctantly began my algebra homework. Talk about *boring*.

The hardest part of being a kid detective is balancing my social life with my cases. Some days were easier than others. On this day it had been extremely difficult. During my classes, I kept wishing the school day away but not for the regular reasons. I was dying to hear what Shane had found out. He would be back from Boston around 5:00. I glanced at my watch, it was 12:10. There was nothing I could do till then, and as hard as it would be, I was not going to think about the case anymore during school. Instead, I would hang out with my friends and enjoy lunch.

At Belltown High lunch was everyone's favorite period. For twenty-eight minutes you could talk to your friends without worrying about a teacher shushing you, and everyone at my table always took advantage of that. Our table was like a world summit meeting, except the topics we tackled were only important to us. There were always two people passionately feuding over their views, and on this day it was Dan "Franco" Francais and Scotty Donovan. They are best friends, but they never seem to agree on anything. Today's important issue: In which cartoon would you rather live—"The Jetsons" or "The Flintstones."

"'The Jetsons' would be much better. They have those sidewalks that you stand on and you don't even have to walk."

Franco took a bite of his second sandwich.

"Just because you're lazy, doesn't mean that makes it a better cartoon." Scotty pointed to Franco's stomach.

"Hey, I need this meat on my bones, if we want to win the division next year." Franco was a guard on the football team.

"OK. Good. You make my point." Scotty smiled.

"How?" echoed Franco, Gina, and Billy McCarthy. As stupid as the topic was, I was interested too.

"Franco, why do you like to eat?"

"'Cause, I love everything about food."

"If you had a choice, would you rather eat a rack of ribs or a pill that tasted and filled you up like a rack of ribs?"

"That's easy. I'd rather have the rack of ribs 'cause I enjoy the whole eating process." We all laughed.

"That's where you prove my point. In "The Jetsons" they take a pill for dinner. Say you want a cheeseburger and fries. You'd have a cheeseburger and fries pill. You never see Fred and Barney eating food pills. No way. That's why, Franco Francais, you would be miserable living in a Jetsons' cartoon." Scotty sat back and acted like he just made the closing statement in a criminal case.

"What do you think, Orville? Do you think I'd be happier living in a Flintstones' cartoon because of the food?" I couldn't believe how serious my friends were taking this. But, I couldn't laugh because I had also been weighing the pros and cons in my head.

"Well, first of all, Scotty gives you a great pro for "The Flintstones." But, he neglects to mention the major con. I know you hate to run and that is what you would have to do if you wanted to drive in "The Flintstones'" era. Not to mention that your feet would be killing you from using them to brake. Who'd want that?"

The table was silent. I had made a major point. I didn't think there would really be a clear decision until Billy McCarthy spoke up. Billy never talked in our summits unless he had the perfect answer.

"The whole concept was already tackled by a cartoon special that had the Flintstones somehow living in the Jetsons' time period for a while, and vice versa. The moral of the cartoon was, there is no place like home. So either way, Franco would be miserable because he wasn't in Belltown."

Billy looked at his watch. "I have to get going though. I have to ask Mr. Reasons a question about the test." Billy began to get up.

"*TEST*!" The rest of us yelled

"Yeah, he mentioned it last week. It's next period."

Last week is a lifetime to high school kids. We all had forgotten. Next period was nine minutes away. The cartoon talk was the past, Mr Reason's algebra test was the future.

We all scurried for notes from Billy, who, even though he was a straight *A* student, claimed he was going to fail. Everyone knows someone like that.

For the next nine minutes we tried making sense of the notes, looking for some sign of hope like prisoners on death row waiting for a reprieve. The bell finally rang and there was nothing Scotty, Franco, or I could do but face our sentence. I wasn't going to do that. My only hope was the nurse's office!

Even though the school nurse, Mrs. Washington suspected foul play, my fake sore throat worked. I had avoided the test. Or did I? When school ended Billy McCarthy informed me that Mr. Reasons decided to give us another day to study. That was uncharacteristic of "Unreasonable" Reasons. So, I really should've hit the books when I got home, and I did for a while, well ...

Anyway, Shane called and told me to be at the police department at 6:00 sharp. I knocked on his door at 5:50.

"Come on in," he hollered.

Walking in, I found Shane flipping through his file cabinet.

"I figured you'd be early," he said, not looking up.

"Well, it was this or study for an algebra test."

Shane moaned. It was the same moan that goes through my head when math is mentioned. Shane finished filing some papers and then shut the cabinet before he settled down and gave me his full attention.

"OK, Orville. Mel called."

"What did he say!" I jumped.

"Calm down. Take a seat and let me finish. He didn't say anything because I wasn't here. I was still driving down from Boston. He left a message. He'll call at 6:00."

"Great."

"When he calls, I'm going to put the phone on conference call so you can listen in." Shane sat on the edge of his desk.

"Thanks, Shane."

"No problem, but I told Mel it was for a drug case I was working on. I mean, think about it, Orville, if he were to find out that I was getting information for you, I don't think he'd be too pleased. Not only that, but I'd also be the laughing stock of my fraternity. You see, Mel and I went to college together."

"Sure, Shane. I understand." Shane had put his neck and reputation on the line for me on more than one occasion and I didn't want to jeopardize that.

"So, you don't want him to know I'm here?"

"No, actually that's OK. We talked a lot about you today and about the other cases. But, about your listening in, I'll handle it my way."

The phone rang and Shane picked it up.

"Hello." He waited a second and then laughed into the receiver. "I told you never to call me that. Hey, I'm going to put you on conference call. There's someone I want to introduce you to." Shane pushed a button.

"Mel, can you hear me?"

"Loud and clear." Mel's voice echoed in the room.

"Good, I want you to meet Orville Jacques."

"The great kid detective. I'm honored."

Shane and I laughed. Mel's voice was warm so just hearing it, I knew he had a great sense of humor.

"Hi, Mel, good to meet you."

"No, it's good to meet you. I guess Belltown's finest, Detective O'Connell, has met his match."

"Mel, Orville wanted to see how two top-notch professionals work. Well, one anyway. So, I thought I'd let him sit in on this one." They both chuckled.

"Well, Orville if you want to learn the trade Leslie O'Connell is the one to teach you."

"*Leslie?*" I whispered to Shane.

"My middle name. Mother's maiden name," he whispered back and waved his hand to drop it.

"And I thought the name *Orville* was bad," I muttered under my breath.

"OK, Mel, whatcha got for me?"

"I won't go into describing the tests that I had the boys in the lab run. You know all about that, Shane. Gotta pen?" Mel asked.

"You know I do, Mel. You're just trying to draw out the suspense for as long as you can."

Mel laughed, "Guilty as charged. Book me, OK. Your mysterious fabric is ... a party dress."

"Party dress?" Shane looked at me and I shrugged.

"Yes, I thought this had to do with a drug case you're working on." Mel's tone was suspicious.

"It does or it might," Shane said.

"Well, is your drug case thirty-five years old? And

how old was the drug dealer, between six and eight?"

"C'mon, Mel, stop talking in riddles and get to the point, will ya?"

"The material is from a child's dress, made for a girl between six and eight. But, the material itself is at least thirty five years old."

Shane had been writing on a piece of paper. He held it up so I could see it. It said: Does any of this make sense?

I shook my head. No.

"Mel, you don't have to tell me how you figured out how old the material was, I know the test they run. But, how on earth did you figure out it was a dress made for a girl between the ages of six and eight?"

"There was a small black *X* on the label. The guys in the lab, I really shouldn't say guys because it was Cindy, she said to say hi and she misses y …"

"Yeah, yeah. Go on." Shane rushed on, and I wondered by his reaction if Cindy was *his X.*

"Well, she found out that the *X* stands for Children's Xtravagant Clothes, expensive clothing made for kids during the sixties. The company operated out of Lowell, Massachusetts. So, if your drug dealer is wearing thirty-five-year-old children's party dresses, you're in for quite a mystery." Mel chuckled.

Shane was biting his lip. I knew he wanted to tell Mel this wasn't a drug case either, but he restrained himself "Well, thanks a lot, Mel."

"No problem. Anything for an old member. We really miss you here. You really should …"

Here? Had Shane been in the FBI?

"Let's not go into that again. OK." What Shane said was not a question—it was an order.

"Orville, you still there?"

"Yes, Mel."

"You can learn a lot from that man. He's solved some cases you wouldn't ..."

"OK. 'Bye, Mel." Shane pushed the button and cut Mel off just as he was saying, "You're not going to hang...

Click. He was gone.

Up on me. Are you? I imagined the rest.

"Did any of that make sense to your case?" Shane peered down at his pad. "About a party dress that's at least thirty-five years old made for a girl between six and eight?"

"No, but at least I know what it is now."

"Tell me what this case is all about?" Shane asked.

I didn't even pause to answer Shane's question but started to rattle off my own list of questions.

"Did you work for the FBI? And tell me about some cases you've solved? And who is Cindy? Your ex-girl-friend?"

"OK. OK. You made your point. I won't ask. But, the first time you think there's trouble, you let me know."

"I will." I paused and smiled. "*Leslie.*"

"Yeah, very funny." He changed the subject quickly, "I never asked you about your trip to Ireland. How was it?"

"Your cousin Colm didn't tell you?" I asked, looking down at my watch: 6:21.

"He called the other day and just told me that you spent many lazy days by the fire drinking tea." Shane squinted.

"If that's what he told you, that's what I did. I gotta get going. Thanks again." I winked and shut the door behind me. I knew Shane O'Connell well enough to know that the wink would make him wonder what kind of trouble I got into over in Ireland. As I headed out of the Belltown Police Department, I wasn't wondering about Ireland and the trouble that was behind me, I was wondering about Belltown and the trouble that was in front of me.

CHAPTER
THREE

I STOPPED AT THE first pay phone I spotted and dropped in a couple of quarters to call Vanessa to fill her in on what I had found out. She had no idea why her father would be afraid of a dress that was thirty-five years old.

"I mean, thirty-five years ago my father was just a kid."

I tucked that thought into the back of my mind, and told her I'd keep in touch. Did this dress and the person who wore it have something to do with Douglas Hyde's childhood? I wondered, as I walked briskly through the frigid winter's night toward Dr. Wilder's house. A morbid thought then struck me. Did this dress have something to do with Elizabeth Hyde's drowning? She was eight years old when she drowned. Maybe, the dress was Douglas Hyde's sister's, and she gave it to his

29

firstborn? That is, if Douglas Hyde had a sister!

"Too much speculation," I said to myself to turn off the different scenarios that were running through my brain. I had to get more pieces before I could attempt the puzzle.

Mrs. Wilder skipped the standard greeting at the door.

"Orville, get in here before you catch a cold. It's freezing out there."

"Hi, Mrs. Wilder. Is Dr. Wilder around?" I blew on my hands while heading straight for the coal stove.

"You don't have gloves?"

"No. I forgot them."

Mrs. Wilder shook her head in admonition and then said, "I'll try to find you an extra pair for the walk home."

"Dave's in the TV room watching the news." She went on her search.

I wandered into the TV room and found Dr. Wilder stretched out in a lounge chair talking to the set.

"For once could you report some good news."

"Hi, Dr. Wilder."

I caught him off guard and he jumped a bit.

"Oh, hi, Orville. You scared me. I was just telling the news guy I'm sick of all the depressing news."

"I agree." I sat down on the sofa.

"So, what can I do for you, Orville. He clicked off the remote and gave me his full attention.

"Well, Dr. Wilder I'm ..."

"Orville, I've told you a million times to call me Dave. I'm a laid-back scientist who's not into titles. The only person I consider a doctor is Dr. J. Do you remember him? He played for the 76ers."

Dave Wilder wasn't into titles because he was still a hippie. He grew up in the sixties and never outgrew it. Neither did his hair! It was still growing. He managed to keep his hair in a ponytail, but his speckled salt and pepper beard was out of control. If you were into stereotyping, you might stereotype him as a bum. Thankfully, my parents weren't into that. Dr. Wilder was not only a brilliant man but a great guy.

"Dr. J. was a little before my time." I knew he retired in the eighties.

"Of course, that's too bad because *there* was a man who could operate. So, what's up? Your dad's still over in Ireland?"

"Yeah, he's going to be teaching over there for two months. That's why I came to you." Nice segue, I thought.

"Well, what do you need?"

"I have to do this paper for my U.S. history class. We had to pick different topics. I thought I'd write mine on Douglas Hyde running for Congress, and I hoped I could get some insights from you since you work at the Belltown Oceanographic."

"I can do you one better. I'll give Doug a call and you can ask him some questions personally." Dr. Wilder reached for the phone. I got nervous. I didn't want to blow my cover,

"That's OK. I'd rather this be an objective piece." I didn't know if that made any sense, but Dr. Wilder seemed to buy it.

"OK. What do you want to ask me?"

"How long have you known Douglas Hyde?"

"Since 1979. That's when I moved to Belltown. Doug was the first friend I made, even before your dad."

My dad and Dr. Wilder met while playing basketball together in a summer league.

"What kind of man would you say he is?"

"Well, he's the best man to represent the Cape. He has ideas that will save our environment and ..."

"Yes, but what kind of man would you say he is?" I pushed.

"Oh," Dr. Wilder was taken aback a little. "He's a complicated man. You see, he's very loyal in the sense that he'd give you the shirt off his back to help you if you were in a jam. But, he doesn't like to get too close to people."

"Why would someone with that kind of personality run for Congress, considering he'd be working with people all the time?" This intrigued me.

"I think part of the answer is the platform he is using—the environment. Sometimes I think he loves working to save the environment more than he loves his own family."

Dr. Wilder sighed.

"So, would you say he's a workaholic?"

"Yes, but he wasn't always. He used to be the first one out of the Oceanographic on a Friday afternoon to be with his wife and kids but..." He paused and wasn't sure if he should reveal any more.

"That's OK. I won't write this in my paper. Y'know,

about his daughter's drowning."

"Right because that's when he changed—when Elizabeth drowned. I'm not a psychologist but when she drowned, I think the pain was too much for Doug so that instead of dealing with it, he shut it off. He was no longer close to his wife and Vanessa. He spent all his time at the Oceanographic. Eventually, his wife couldn't take it anymore and divorced him."

"Why didn't she keep custody of Vanessa?" I asked.

"I really don't know why she didn't take Vanessa with her. I'm sure Vanessa, that poor girl, wonders that too." He rubbed his beard in thought.

"How did..." I didn't want my next question to him to sound callous.

"Elizabeth drown?"

"Yes."

"It was an unseasonably hot day in May. Doug had left work early to pick up Elizabeth from school. He told me that he was going to spend the whole day with her. Take her out for an ice cream. Go for a swim. You know that kind of dad and daughter stuff. You know how it is when your parents surprise you and pick you up early from school. It's a great feeling."

"Yeah," I said softly, remembering a time when my dad showed up at my sixth-grade class clutching two tickets to the Red Sox.

"Well." Dr. Wilder stopped. His eyes were filling up.

"I'm sorry, I shouldn't have asked you. I don't need to know that much." I felt guilty for causing his reaction.

"It's OK, Orville. It's just that I was there when Doug

found out his little girl had drowned."

"What do you mean?" I was in shock.

"He told me that they'd end up at Breakers Beach. So, I decided to head down there and go for a swim too. It's great to go down there that early in May because the tourists still haven't arrived. It's always deserted. Well, when I got there, I saw Doug was asleep, lying on his towel soaking up the sun. I woke him and asked where Elizabeth was. I don't want to go into details, but Elizabeth had gone swimming without Doug's knowing and ... when Elizabeth was eventually found by divers it was too late. Doug went into shock, a complete trance. He kept saying it over and over again." Dr. Wilder closed his eyes.

"Saying what?" I asked softly.

"Theresa, not again. Not again."

"Theresa, not again. What did that mean?"

Dr. Wilder opened his eyes and looked over at me, "I don't know what it meant. He was in shock, and because of it, he probably forgot Elizabeth's name." Dr. Wilder looked for the logical explanation.

"Orville, it probably meant nothing."

"Or everything," I whispered to myself as Mrs. Wilder appeared with a pair of gloves.

In the half hour I was in Dr. Wilder's house, the temperature outside had dropped at least ten degrees. It felt like snow was in the air, and we didn't need any more snow considering there were still piles of it on the sidewalk from the last storm. I decided it was easier walking in the street, since I didn't have any drifts to contend with. My whole body was cold except my mind, which was burning with questions. "Theresa, not again." What did it mean? Who was Theresa? Did she really exist? Was the lavender dress hers? What did she have to do with Douglas Hyde's running for Congress? Why would it frighten him?

I knew there was only one person who could answer these questions: Douglas Hyde. I had to talk to him and find some answers. If I found the answers to these questions, I would have a better chance at finding out who was threatening him. My major concern was would Douglas Hyde tell me. I had to find out a way that I could meet him one-on-one and get to the bottom of it all. I needed a plan. A noise behind me distracted my thinking. I thought the noise sounded like a car engine. I looked back and expected to see distant headlights—nothing. Just me and the black night. I wish there were some lights on this street, or even a moon to guide me, I thought. The moon had taken the night off. I continued on, but paranoia was now gripping me. I picked up my pace while straining my ears to listen for the sound. I heard it again. I swung my head back—no car. I could've sworn it sounded like a car traveling at a slow rate of speed.

"It must be a fishing boat's engine," I said, looking at the Belltown harbor, which was fifty yards away. But, the harbor was to my right; the sound was behind me, I realized. The slow engine sound suddenly revved. I snapped my head back. I didn't see anything but the roaring engine told me it was headed my way. "No headlights!" My voice yelled what my brain had just put together. I lunged off the street and landed in a snowdrift just as a truck zoomed by. I wiped myself off and then shook my head as I got up, "Drunk driver."

The red brake lights then lit up the night. The truck stopped for a second, and the sound of gears shifting puzzled me for a moment until I realized the truck was turning around. The driver flipped on the high beams and a floodlight blinded me. He peeled out and started barreling down the road in my direction. This was no drunk driver! The driver was deliberately trying to hit me! But, I couldn't move because a ten-foot snowdrift was between me and the sidewalk.

I desperately tried climbing over the drift, but I kept slipping and falling down. The driver must have known he had time because he screeched to a stop about twenty feet away and unhooked the snowplow, which was in front of the truck. I turned back to the snowdrift. My mind said to stay calm and keep climbing, but the sound of my heart was almost as loud as the engine. As I got closer to the top, the engine revved faster and the plow grated into the street. I finally managed to get to the top of the snowdrift. I stood up and was about to jump over it, but curiosity made me look back. Sparks flew from the plow as it ranked the street, headed for my snowdrift. It sounded like a fingernail on a chalkboard, but I knew the plow would do more damage than just make me cringe.

Sweat poured off my brow and instantly froze in the night as I leaped off. I landed hard on the ground and felt a tremendous force push me about five feet. It was the plow pushing the snowdrift. I finally came to a stop, but I knew it would be brief. I heard the truck backing up. The driver was going to hit the snowdrift again. I knew the mountain of snow would collapse and bury me. I had to get up and run or I wouldn't be found till spring! I hopped to my feet and bolted. The driver must have spotted me with the floodlight because the truck stopped plowing and raced after me. Before I knew it, the floodlight was on my shoulders, and I was sprinting straight toward the harbor.

"What am I going to do?" the voice in my head yelled as I came to the dock at the edge of the harbor. I stared down at the lapping murky water and then back at the blinding white lights. I was trapped. There was nowhere to go except …

The impact from the jarring ice-cold harbor water was unbearable. I gasped hard and fast for breath. It came in spurts. I could almost feel my face turning blue as I treaded water and squinted to focus for a harbor ladder. I couldn't see any.

In fact, I couldn't see much of anything. I felt my face with my numb right hand and realized I had forgotten to take my glasses off when I jumped into the water. They were gone, and my eyesight without them was beyond blurry. I had to stay in control. There was no time to panic. If I didn't swim somewhere fast, I knew the temperature would send me into hypothermia. Luckily, I had experience in swimming in these conditions.

"What do I do now? ... Look for a light." I said to myself, and seconds later spotted a glowing light. I swam the crawl as hard as I could toward the yellow beam. I was getting closer to the light when I realized my winter coat was dragging me down. I unzipped the coat and let the water swallow it before I continued. As I got closer to the light I was barely able to make it out, but I did. It was the harbor ladder attached to the dock. It dipped into the piercing cold water surrounded by a halo of light. I grabbed the ladder and pulled my weak body up the steps, one by one, gasping in relief. I almost reached the top, where the harbor and parking lot join, when a question pounded in my head. How was the ladder lit up? There are no lights at this end of the harbor.

I stopped climbing and tried to listen above the foghorn and my chattering teeth. It was a faint sound— a click. But, it spoke volumes. I knew the clicking sound was a gun being cocked. It was a trap! The truck hadn't left.

The driver had shined the floodlight on the harbor ladder and was waiting for me. He was either going to shoot me like a tin duck at the county fair, or he was going to force me back into the harbor and let Mother Nature do his dirty work for him. I stared back down at the bone-chilling water, and I knew I had no choice but to dive back in, and swim to the other side of the harbor. I said a quick prayer to God hoping it wasn't a suicide mission, and I wasn't going to end up buried in a gloomy ocean grave. I dove off the ladder, and was struck immediately by the needle-sharp coldness of the water. I began the crawl and then went into the breaststroke. I could feel a light on me. He had found me with his floodlight and was going to follow me as far as the beam could travel. Whoever he was, he was probably having his kicks watching me flail away, I thought. This gave me the drive to continue.

Eventually, I swam out of the light's reach. I felt like I would be out of everyone's reach if I continued. My legs and arms were weak. I could hardly move them. More than anything, the sound of a bell almost did me in. It was the bell attached to the buoy that signifies the middle of the harbor. I had only gone halfway. My purple fingers grabbed onto the buoy, and I laughed lightly at the horrible irony. Less than a week ago, I had cheated death in a raging sea in Ireland only to come home and be devoured by the Belltown harbor; the harbor where fathers showed their sons how to bait hooks, where teenagers hung out on a boring Saturday night, and where locals mockingly waved at the tourists on the *Island Princess*. My life was going to be snatched from the harmless Belltown harbor, and the last sound I would hear was the swinging bell.

It was just too ironic. I couldn't let this happen, but there was nothing else I could do. I was losing my grip on the buoy. There was no way I could make it to the other side of the harbor. My hopes were sinking and I knew soon I would too, when suddenly it appeared. Even I, with my poor vision recognized it—a fishing boat entering the harbor. I figured I had to swim ten yards to get in the boats lane, and then maybe I could cling onto something, anything. It was my last chance. Normally, ten yards would have taken seconds, but my arms were like a boxer's in the twelfth round. The boat was approaching fast, and if I was a few seconds late in its lane it would be my last few seconds. My mind was getting cloudy so I kicked harder; I had to fight it. I reached the boat's lane just in time to feel a net hanging over the side. I clutched the net and held on as tightly as my sagging arms and stiff fingers would let me as the net dragged me toward the other side of the harbor. I ignored the head rush of frigid pain, knowing I was almost safe.

The boat finally docked. I tried lifting myself onto the deck, but all my energy was spent. After all I had been through, I wasn't going to make it. A blurry vision appeared yelling something at me I didn't understand. Then everything became just one large blur that faded suddenly into blackness.

CHAPTER
FOUR

"I DIDN'T KNOW YOU were in the Belltown Polar Bear Club," said a familiar voice. I rubbed my eyes and tried to make out the figure of a man hovering above me.

"What?" I managed.

"The polar bear club. I mean, they're the only people who swim in these conditions." The man laughed and I was finally able to place him.

"Shane, what are you doing here? And where is *here*?" I felt a hot-wet senssation on my forehead and realized it was a steaming facecloth.

"You're aboard the *Mary Five*," said another voice from the other room.

"The *Mary Five*?" I was confused.

"I named my first boat after my girlfriend Mary about forty years ago. The boat sank about a hundred miles off the coast of Nantucket, just about the same time ol' Mary sank me for some Wall Street banker." The man laughed and Shane joined in. A second later, the man appeared with a mug in his hands and said, "Drink this. It will squeeze the harbor water out of your bones."

"Thank you ..." I propped myself up in the tiny bunk and cradled the mug.

"Orville, this is the man who pulled you out of the water, Mr. Bedford," Shane said.

"Mr. Bedford, I can't thank you enough. I owe you my life." I put out my hand.

"Please, call me Clarence," he said and shook my hand. It was a fisherman's hand. Leathery. Weathered.

"Clarence, how can I ever repay you?" I asked.

"Repay me? That's silly talk, Orville. All I did was give you a hand."

"But ..." I began to interrupt.

"Wait. I know how you can repay me. Drink what's in the mug."

I took a sip of the drink and almost gagged. Shane and Clarence laughed.

"What is this ... this ..."

"There are some things in life you shouldn't ask questions about." Clarence chuckled and then turned to Shane. "Detective O'Connell, I'll go on the deck so you can have some privacy.

"Thank you, Clarence." Shane's tone got serious.

"Yes." I was about to say thank you, but Clarence had disappeared.

"Orville, what happened?"

"Well...

I told Shane everything about the chase, and was thinking about spilling my guts and telling him that it must have something to do with the Hyde case, when he dropped a bomb on me.

"I'm just glad Clarence found my card in your wallet and called me first. There's something I've got to tell you." All the laughter was gone from Shane's voice.

"What?"

"A little birdie called me about ten minutes before I got Clarence's call. Said that a hit had been ordered on the kid detective."

"A hit," I said in disbelief. I had heard the phrase in a thousand movies, but I never dreamed it would ever apply to me!

"Yeah. He said it had to do with one of the guys you helped put away. But, he didn't say which one or which case.

"Oh my God!" I shook my head and took another sip but this time didn't even notice the bad seaweed taste.

"I think you better stay at my place tonight."

"Tonight?" I looked at my watch—8:27. I couldn't believe it was still working. "Oh man, my mom's gonna—" I paused and was about to say kill me but thought better of it, "—be mad. I was supposed to be home hours ago."

"I'll call her and tell her you're with me, hanging

out at my house, working on a paper for your crime class, and lost track of time. Tomorrow we have to inform her about what's really going on."

"Shane." He retreated before I could protest. What is *really* going on was the question I pondered. Yes, the hit could have been ordered because of one of the other cases I had solved. There was no doubt there were some powerful people behind iron bars because of my curiosity and luck at uncovering their sordid secrets. But, the little voice in my head that always goes against all logic was speaking to me. It said, "This has something to do with the Hyde case." I knew, however, irrational as that voice sounded, I was going to listen to it. I had to. Before I accepted Shane's theory, I had to find out more about Douglas Hyde.

When we got to Shane's house, I told him I was exhausted. He said I could sleep on the pull-out couch in his den. I knew he had a phone in the den so I gave a fake yawn and waved goodnight. I called Gina and asked her if she could pick me up at Shane's for school in the morning. No problem. The problem was Shane allowing Gina to drive me to school. I figured my argument would work. I would tell him that if there was a hit out on me, we wouldn't want the person to know the police had found out or the assassin would never be captured. Plus the fact, would he really try to kill me in broad daylight? I wondered. I gulped. What if he did? I had to take a chance. I needed Gina to drive me to Douglas Hyde's house, and I didn't want Shane to find out. I had something to deliver. It was something that would get the ball rolling. I scanned his den for the things I needed to make for my delivery: scissors—on the desk; tape and paper—in the desk; magazines—a stack of old *Sports Illustrated* magazines were scattered on a coffee table.

I cut up the old magazines and taped the different sized letters on a piece of typing paper. When I finished clipping and taping the letter read:

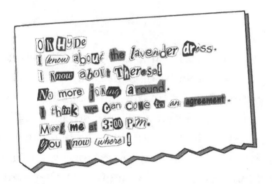

> OK Hyde
> I (know) about the lavender dress.
> I know about Theresa!
> No more joking around.
> I think we can come to an agreement.
> Meet me at 3:00 P.m.
> You know (where)!

It seemed to take forever to cut out the different letters and I realized why kidnappers usually get to the point with their ransom notes. I did get lucky though when I cut out a whole word—*agreement.* Some baseball player had signed a three-year multimillion dollar agreement. When I finished putting my letter together I finally went to bed. Sleep was another matter. I was still a little shaken from my ordeal. I turned the light on and read the letter again. I knew I was just playing on the hunch that there was really a Theresa and she had something to do with the lavender dress, which had petrified Douglas Hyde. If I went with that hunch, I figured I'd take it one step farther: "You know where to meet." He might have no clue as to where to meet, but I figured that he would go to the place of whomever he thought was behind the blackmailing, and I would either confront him or spy on him. I just hoped my figuring was better in detective work than it was in algebra. There was certainly a lot more at stake than just a passing grade!

My argument with Shane worked. Well, for the most part, anyway. Gina did spot Officer Jameson tailing us in an old beat-up Buick. She put her truck into four-wheel drive and headed down a private street, one the town wasn't responsible for plowing. Even though the last snowstorm was four days ago, the road was still impassable except for Gina's four-wheel drive. That made sense since all the houses were summer houses. I looked back and saw a cloud of smoke rising in the distance followed by Officer Jameson jumping out and kicking the rusted old Buick and then waving a fist at us. He had put it all together that we deliberately went that way. Gina and I laughed. It felt good to laugh, considering what I had been through. The laughter suddenly died when we came to Douglas Hyde's house. I hopped out and looked into the newspaper tube for the paper.

"Cape Cod Times. Perfect." I put the letter in be-

tween the sports page and the obituaries and jumped back into the truck. A part of me felt really bad that Mr. Hyde was going to be greeted with the letter. But, if he wasn't going to tell his own daughter what the threat was, he certainly wasn't going to spill his guts to some nosy teenager. Scare tactics were my only hope. We drove to my house and I grabbed my spare glasses and another winter coat. I kept wondering if I had done something terribly wrong, but my guilt faded when I analyzed the greater purpose—I wanted to help Douglas Hyde, not hurt him.

At lunch everybody but me was discussing the topic of the day: What is the most predictable TV rerun? *"The Love Boat,"* Gina said. They meet. They fall in love. They get into an argument but then the crew fixes it. It's so cheesy but romantic. I love it."

Everyone at the table laughed except me. I kept thinking about my letter and about 3:00.

"Orville, what's wrong?" Billy McCarthy asked.

I shook my head, nothing.

"He's probably nervous about the test," Scotty answered.

Test. The word floored me. I had forgotten about the algebra test again. I leaped out of my chair and hurried over to Mary Joyce's table, leaving the others shaking their heads in bewilderment.

"Mary, I need a favor."

"Orville, I can't do that for you again." Mary knew exactly what I needed. Mary could do the best impersonation of her mother, the receptionist for my dentist. I handed her a quarter and pleaded and pleaded till the bell rang. It was hopeless. I was going to have to face Mr. Reasons.

It was Christmas all over again for Mr. Reasons as he handed me my test and smiled. "I held off giving the test to the class yesterday. Knowing you were so ill, I wanted you to have a chance to take it with your classmates."

"Yeah, whatever," I mumbled in defeat.

Gina suddenly appeared at the door with a note.

"Miss Goldman, my former prize student, what are you doing here?"

"I have a note from the school secretary." Mr. Reasons went over and took the note and read it. His smile vanished and he slowly raised his head.

"Mr. Jacques, it seems you're being dismissed for a dental appointment." He crumpled up the note and dropped it into the basket.

I bit the side of my mouth trying to hold back my smile.

I owed Mary Joyce. She came through for me in the clutch.

"Since it's Friday, you can make up the test Monday

after school." His voice was barely audible.

"OK. Gee, but, I really wanted to take it today." I turned back and winked at Scotty and Billy. They gave me gotta-give-you-credit smiles, and I headed out the door past a sullen Mr. Reasons.

Mary Joyce not only came through for me, but she also had Gina dismissed. Apparently, the favor Mary granted was only because Gina asked her after I had gone to class.

"So, why did you have Mary dismiss you too?" I asked Gina after we pulled out of the Belltown High parking lot.

"Why not?" She laughed for a second, "Orville, do you really think I'm going to let you follow Hyde on your own?"

"Gina, don't even think..." I began.

"Mary owed me a huge favor and I used it for you. I just hooked you up big time so now you owe me." Gina looked determined.

"But Gina ..." I tried to object.

"No, I'm coming with you. Anyway, how are you going to follow him? On your mountain bike?" Gina put on her right blinker, and drove down the street that would eventually lead us to the Belltown Oceanographic. I didn't say a word. I had no argument. I had never thought about how I would tail Hyde. Since I didn't have my license, there would be a lot of peddling to do, especially if he headed off Cape.

"Orville, quick. Wake up," Gina said in a hushed whisper while tugging at my arm.

"What? Where am I? What time is it?" I shot up in the passenger seat. I didn't even think to look at my watch.

"Get down! You don't want him to see you," Gina ordered. I was about to ask who when I caught a glimpse of Douglas Hyde unlocking his car. I did as Gina ordered, but I was still a little dazed until Gina answered all my questions.

"It's 2:48. You fell asleep about a half hour ago," Gina said while keeping her eyes on Hyde who was pulling out of the parking lot.

"I can't believe I fell asleep." I stretched.

"I can. Your body is still recovering from your ordeal last night. But, I wouldn't want you on a stakeout. My disco didn't even wake you." Gina had given Hyde about a fifteen second lead before she started her truck and put it into drive.

"Well, we know one thing for sure," I said as we stayed about five-car lengths behind him.

"What's that?"

"He's not going off Cape because he only has eleven minutes to get to the meeting place."

Gina shook her head in agreement and we didn't talk for the next eight minutes. Hyde was driving in the direction of West Belltown.

What could be there? I wondered. Suddenly Hyde turned into a dirt driveway by the old Belltown railroad tracks. Gina slammed on her brakes and gave me a look.

I shrugged. "I have no idea why he's parking by the old railroad tracks."

Gina realized she was in the middle of the road and she should park somewhere fast before Hyde spotted us. She fiddled with the gearshift and then drove over a small hill of snow, and we were hidden behind the snow-weighted trees. It was the perfect hiding place. We had a clear view of Hyde getting out of his car. He had a worried look on his face as his head bobbed back and forth in search of his blackmailer. Then he turned from our direction and walked on the tracks through the snow.

"Now what?" Gina asked.

"What do you mean?" My heart was jumping a bit.

"Well, your letter didn't work. There are no houses or businesses by those tracks. So, your theory of Mr. Hyde going straight to the person who he thinks might be the blackmailer goes right out the window."

"Yes that's true, but why did he think the blackmailer would meet him by the old Belltown railroad tracks?"

"I don't know. Why?" Gina asked while keeping her eyes on Hyde.

"That's what I'm going to find out." I leaped out of the truck and shut the door before Gina could argue. I darted behind trees and bushes that ran parallel to the tracks until I found Douglas Hyde sitting on an icy rail and crying like a helpless child. I wasn't expecting this,

I thought. What do I do? There was no time to think of the proper way to introduce myself as I appeared from behind the trees.

"Mr. Hyde."

He snapped his head up. His eyes were swollen.

"Why are you doing this?" He jumped to his feet and charged. He grabbed my arm and shook me.

"Wait! I'm here to help."

"Help? Help? You've sent me threatening letters, and you say you're here to help?" He shook me one final time and threw me to the ground.

"You don't understand..." I wiped myself off.

"You're darn right I..."

"Vanessa hired me," I jumped in. He was taken aback.

"Vanessa, what? What's going on? Make sense. Now! First of all, who are you?"

"My name is Orville Jacques."

"Oh, my God. I know who you are." He was putting it all together, shaking his head. I knew what he was thinking: Orville Jacques, the kid detective.

"You wouldn't tell Vanessa why you were being blackmailed so she hired me to find out. The letter you got this morning isn't from the real blackmailer. It was from me."

"Why did you send it?" He was confused.

"I had to get some answers, and I had to get you alone. So, I wrote down what I knew."

Hyde calmed down and said, "Look, Orville, I appreciate that you are trying to help my daughter, but this should be none of Vanessa's concern and it should certainly be none of yours."

"Sir, how can you think it's none of Vanessa's concern. She receives a threatening letter about her father and she is supposed to forget it? And I know what you're thinking about me. He's just a kid. Well, did you ever stop to think how this kid found out that the piece of fabric Vanessa gave me was a lavender-colored party dress?"

Hyde gave me a look of how-did-you-know-that.

"Also, I was forced into the Belltown harbor last night by some whacko with a gun, and I think it has something to do with all of this. Whatever *this* is. So, I think you owe me a few answers." I knew that would shake him.

"Someone tried to kill you!" Mr. Hyde's eyes grew wide.

"Yes, but let's talk about you. What is the threat about, Mr. Hyde?" I persisted.

"I figured you knew, considering the letter you sent about Theresa."

"No, that was just a hunch. I found out you mentioned Theresa's name the day your daughter drowned."

"How did you find that..."

"The point is I did. And I'll find out the rest even if you won't tell me. Come on, Mr. Hyde, I want to help." I had to be firm.

Hyde paused for a long, hard moment and then said, "OK. I'll tell you. It all happened May 4, 1962. I had just turned eight years old the week before. I was an only child, and my parents were always working. My best friend was Theresa Bigelow."

Theresa. The name made my spine tingle.

"May fourth was Theresa's birthday. She also turned eight. I wasn't invited to her party because Theresa's father didn't like me. The Bigelows were a rich family who owned a clothing mill in Lowell."

"Children's Xtravagant Clothes," I blurted out, remembering the party dress.

"Yes, how did..." He stopped when he knew I wouldn't answer the question. "Well, Mr. Bigelow thought I was a bad influence on Theresa because when we played she was never ladylike. We would do things like catch frogs and climb trees."

"What did Theresa's mother think about having a tomboy for a daughter?"

"Mrs. Bigelow had died the previous summer after a fall off the Belltown Heights Hill when she was taking a walk."

"Oh." I nodded for him to continue. I figured I'd better stop interrupting him.

"The night of the party, I went over to Theresa's house. She was wearing a brand new party dress her father had given her, and was entertaining some snobby, rich girls by the pool. She looked bored and when no one was looking, I threw a penny in her direction to get her attention. She picked it up and walked over to the bushes. When she came to the bushes she lifted the penny and said, 'Let's go have some fun.' I lit two sparklers, and gave her one and we laughed and walked until we got here." He was filling up again.

"Then what happened?"

"She was so young. Just like my little girl Elizabeth." He wasn't listening to me.

"Tell me what happened, Mr. Hyde." I tried to be as gentle as I could.

"Putting a penny on the track to flatten it was our favorite thing to do. We did that at least four nights a week in the summer. We would put the penny on the track and then hide in those bushes, and watch the train whiz by. We would make up stories pretending we were on the train going to different parts of the world. That night ... a train was coming and Theresa's shoe got caught or something, and I guess I must have fainted in fright. I don't know. I don't remember. All I remember is waking up in my bed and my parents telling me that Theresa had been hit by a train." Mr. Hyde wiped his tears away with his sleeve, "Then they told me she had died."

"It was an accident. Why would someone blackmail you for that?"

"Was it? No one knows for sure if it was an accident. Rumors began. One was that I watched and didn't help. Some even said I pushed her. But, I honestly don't know what happened. I have no memory of it. The rumors started again about me when Elizabeth drowned. I went into shock. It was like I was reliving both tragedies at once. Not many know this, but I spent two months in a mental hospital after Elizabeth drowned. The blackmailer knows, though. He seems to know everything. Vanessa received the third letter. The first came with a flattened penny, and said something to the effect that it wasn't very lucky for Theresa. The second one said something like 'psycho for congressman.'"

"There is no proof that you did anything wrong."

"Orville, these days speculation is more powerful than proof. I really thought I had put all of this behind me. What a fool I was to think I could run for office and none of this would come out." He shook his head slowly.

"It still might not come out. Have you thought of having the police look into the situation? " I was trying to give him some sign of hope.

"There are leaks to the press in every department. I am seriously thinking of dropping out of the race."

"That's your decision, Mr. Hyde. But, there is one thing you have to do. You have to tell Vanessa the truth. She loves you and she deserves some answers. It will explain a great deal to her. She wonders why you two aren't close. I would think it would be difficult for you to get close for fear you might lose her too."

"You're right. And I was going to tell her when I got some answers myself. You see, my therapist suggested that I see a hypnotist. She felt it was my only hope for remembering, so I've gone twice. The hypnotist has been slowly bringing me along and at my next appointment she is going to have me go over the day of the party. I hope to find out that I fainted and didn't just sit and watch. That's when I thought I'd tell Vanessa, but you made a good point today. She shouldn't be going to bed in fear. I do love her."

"Mr. Hyde, if you decide to involve the police, I have a friend on the force who you could trust to be discreet."

"Thank you ... Orville. Thank you for listening. I'll think about it." He shook my hand.

"Well, I'm sorry I had to bring you back here."

"Ironically, the hypnotist told me to come here before my next visit. She said it might jar some memories."

"Did it?"

"No, just a feeling. A feeling of being trapped in complete fear."

Mr. Hyde put his head down and slowly edged along the tracks. I thought having my questions answered would close a lot of doors. The answers just opened more.

CHAPTER
FIVE

WHEN MY SLEUTHING uncovers a secret, I usually have a feeling of satisfaction. I didn't have that feeling about the Douglas Hyde case. In fact, I felt lousy that I had put him in the position where he had to face his past tragedies. I also didn't feel too great because Shane was upset at me for ditching Officer Jameson and then getting dismissed from school early without notifying him. He threatened to tell my mom about the death threat, but fortunately he still listened to reason. I told him my mom would freak out and call my dad and then he would hop on the first plane out of Ireland. He agreed not to tell Mom as long as I promised to let Officer Jameson keep his eye on me. I promised. I may be a lot of things but I'm not stupid. I put on a Fatwall Jack CD, stretched out on my bed, and was about to escape to the bluesy voice of Miss Erica Rodney when the phone rang.

"Hello," I said into the receiver.

"Hi, Orville."

"Yeah."

"It's Vanessa."

"Oh, hi, Vanessa." I didn't know what to do. She had hired me to find out about her father, but I felt it was his duty to tell her about his past. Not mine.

"I just called to thank you."

"Thank me?"

"Yes, I just had a long talk with my dad. He told me how you confronted him today."

"Oh, he did?" I was relieved. I was off the hook.

"Yeah, he told me everything. We both had a good cry, and shared a lot of our feelings. I have you to thank for that."

"Well, I don't know about that. I think your dad was going to tell you soon."

"Yes, maybe, but you made soon become today..." She paused, "I'm also calling to invite you to Pilgrim Pond tomorrow night."

"What for?"

"I convinced my dad not to drop out of the race, and everything is going on as planned." She assumed I knew what she was talking about.

"Planned?"

"Oh, I guess you haven't heard about the skating party. My dad is going to give a speech, then I'm going to skate a program, and then the rest of the skating club and public will join in."

"Sounds like fun."

"Yeah, it's going to be great. We're going to have torches all around the edge of the pond and a tent with hot drinks and desserts. Can you come?" She sounded excited.

"Yeah, I'd love to. Hey, Vanessa, I don't mean to bring you down, but I have a few questions about the case."

"What?" Her voice dropped a bit.

I picked up the paper and looked at the name. "I'm such an amateur, I never asked you about Barry Field, the guy your dad is running against. Do you think he's capable of blackmail?"

"No, my dad and he differ on some issues like the environment, but for the most part their views are similar, and they get along pretty well for two guys who want the same job. I'm almost positive he has nothing to do with it."

"OK. What about enemies? I know I should've asked you this earlier. Does he have any?"

"He doesn't have one in the world. Hey, I really have to get going, Orville. The party starts at 6:00. Bring anyone you want.

"What about issues? Are there any..."

"Orville, I'm very grateful for what you did, and now it's up to my dad to decide if he wants the police involved. I'll send you the gift certificates for the CDs I owe you, and as far as I'm concerned the case I gave you is solved." She said it kind of harshly and then added, "I don't want you to get hurt. I'll see you tomorrow night."

"Yeah. Vanessa, one other thing."

"What's that?"

"You called your father Dad."

"I know. It feels great. It really feels great. Bye."

I had felt lousy, but Vanessa's phone call and the sound of joy in her voice reminded me why I love what I do. The next night would be the perfect opportunity to find out more pieces to the puzzle. I had spent all my time concentrating on Douglas Hyde, but now I had to shift gears and look into Barry Field, possible enemies, and issues. As far as Vanessa was concerned, my job was over. As far as I was concerned, well you know...

There hadn't been a break in the cold spell that visited Belltown. In fact, the weather forecasters were still whispering that a nor'easter might hit us. I never put much faith in weather forecasters. They have let me down on many a school day, so they weren't going to stop me from going to Pilgrim Pond.

I invited Gina to go to the skating party, and emphasized that she let Vanessa know that Gina and I weren't a couple. She laughed. "Like I'd really want people to think that."

Gina understood, though, people always assumed we were a couple just because we hung out. We learned this when Henry Hampshire, a guy Gina liked, approached me one night and asked me how serious Gina and I were.

I filled good ol' Henry in and Gina and he ended up going out for a couple of months. I was hoping Gina would say the same to Vanessa, and who knows? I had been thinking about Vanessa a lot and it wasn't just because of the case. When we arrived at Pilgrim Pond there was a roped-off area where cars could park. Gina backed in to park and as I jumped out of her truck, I almost bumped into the person getting out of the car to my right.

"Sorry," I said, not looking up.

"Orville, you made it," said Vanessa Hyde. She had her long blonde hair in a ponytail and was wearing a white headband to keep the hair out of her deep blue eyes.

"Oh ... yeah," I managed. We were inches away from each other, and I realized I had a feeling in my stomach that I hadn't had since Maria Simpkins—the good sick feeling. I wasn't positive but I sensed that's how she felt too. Of course, I could've been wrong. It wouldn't have been the first time!

"Well, I'm glad." I think that's what Vanessa said as she stood there staring into my eyes with her skates draped over her shoulders.

"Hi, you must be Vanessa." Gina came over from behind the truck.

"Yes, you're..." I don't want to sound cocky, but I thought I saw a slight frown appear on Vanessa's face.

"Gina Goldman. I'm here with Orville"—Gina allowed me to stew for a second and my eyes pleaded with her— "as one of his best friends who's here to support Douglas Hyde's run for Congress."

"Oh, great. I'm glad you could come, Gina." Vanessa brightened up and shook Gina's hand.

"I just hope Ms. Goldman is eighteen. I could use all the votes I can get." Mr. Hyde laughed and came over to us.

"I'm sorry, sir, I have at least a year and a half to go. But, I am honored to meet you. I have been following your campaign in the papers. It's wonderful how much you care about the environment."

"Thank you, I really..." Mr. Hyde stopped and spotted something in the snow-covered bushes. He went over to the bushes and pulled out three empty plastic jugs. We moved closer and watched as he read out loud what the labels said: Antifreeze-No-Name Brand.

"Litter bugs." He shook his head and took a plastic bag out of his pocket, opened it, and threw the three bottles into the bag.

"Do you always carry a plastic bag with you?" I asked.

"Never leave home without it. We better get down to the festivities, gang." I was glad to see that his mood was a lot happier than the previous day.

Gina whispered in my ear, "That environmental stuff isn't just all talk. He's the real McCoy."

I nodded in agreement while checking out the scene. The scene reminded me of how New England was portrayed in the old black and white movies—an old-fashioned feeling. There were torches jammed into the snow by the edge of the pond that provided the lighting. People were scattered everywhere but most of them were under a blue tent. And for good reason. I figured that was where all the food and beverages were. There were probably close to a hundred people milling about, but what struck me as odd was that no one was skating on the pond.

"Vanessa, I thought this was a skating party?"

"It is. Here." She handed me a program before she suddenly got lost with her father in the sea of well-wishers who ushered them into the tent.

I read the program to Gina:

Pilgrim Pond Family Skating Party

Place: Pilgrim Pond, Belltown, Cape Cod

Time: 6:00 PM

List of events: 1. Greeting by candidate for Congress, Douglas Hyde. 2. Vanessa Hyde skates program 3. Belltown Skating Club skates finale. 4. Family skating party (so please stay off the ice until programs are finished). Refreshments will be served in the blue tent.

"Well, I guess I know where we're going." Gina laughed.

"You got that right. I could do with some hot chocolate." I followed Gina's lead into the blue tent where about forty people were drinking hot chocolate and munching on food. I grabbed a hot chocolate and two glazed doughnuts and went to work.

"We should've called Franco." Gina pointed to the feast.

"If we did, this party would already be over." I laughed.

"Testing ... One-two-three. Can you folks hear me?"

A man asked while tapping lightly on the microphone on the podium. Everyone nodded yes.

"Good. I won't go into a long speech except to say, ladies and gentlemen, your next congressman, Douglas Hyde."

Everyone clapped, but it was kind of muffled because we all were wearing mittens and gloves so a couple of people made up for that by yelling at the top of their lungs.

"Thank you. Thank you." Mr. Hyde gave a you-can-stop-clapping hand signal. "I just want to thank everyone who came out tonight during this cold snap. I'm not going to give a long speech about why I'm running for Congress, you folks know what I'm all about. This event is what I'm all about—a family skating party—enjoying the environment with your children and preserving it so some day your children can enjoy it with their children." He paused while cheers and clapping echoed through the tent.

"In the 1620s, the Pilgrims came forty miles every summer from Plymouth to enjoy this pond. Don't we owe it to our future generations to have the same right and the same experience?" More clapping.

"Then, why is it, tonight in the dead of winter, I find trash near this pond." He lifted the garbage bag so everyone could see. There was silence.

"I'll tell you why. Because some people aren't concerned about the dangers to our environment. If you elect me to Congress, it will be my duty to make sure people in Washington will not only be concerned, but they will do something about it!"

There was thunderous applause for a few seconds.

"Now, on a more personal note. I would like to thank my daughter Vanessa. Tonight's event was Vanessa's idea. I want to thank her for that ... but ... more importantly..." He paused and motioned for Vanessa to come to his side. She came and he put his arm around her.

"I want to thank Vanessa for never giving up on me as her father. There were times she probably thought I took her love for granted. I didn't. It is what keeps me going through the tough times." He hugged her and there were smiles and clapping, but my smile had a far greater appreciation of the situation.

Mr. Hyde turned back to the audience. "OK, this is my daughter's show so this proud dad will give her the floor."

Vanessa wiped her eyes dry, smiled, and took over, "I guess at this time I would like to invite everyone to go outside. The focus of my skating program is to honor Mother Earth. The background music I'll be using is by Enya, and I'd especially like to thank 92.7 WMVY. Their van is outside, and will be providing the music all night."

Everyone cheered and then headed out of the tent. In my mind it was already a successful event. Of course, there was a reporter who wasn't affected by the moment. He took pictures and was firing questions at Mr. Hyde.

"Mr. Hyde, you propose the closing down of Fisherman's Banks for six years. You say you want to save the environment, but I guess you don't want to save the fishermen? People say the fishermen will be the endangered species. How do you respond to that?"The young reporter practically shoved a microphone into Mr. Hyde's mouth.

"Look, I've answered that question a million times. I'm aware that many fishermen will lose jobs. I am sorry for that, but if we don't do this now—ten years from now there won't be any fishing jobs to come back to because there won't be any fish. Consequently, there won't be any fishermen."

"So, you're saying..." The reporter began but Mr. Hyde stopped him. "Young man, my daughter is about to do her program. I don't want to miss that. Give my office a call and I promise you we'll get together and I'll be glad to answer any topics about Fisherman's Banks or any other questions you care to discuss."

The reporter changed his tone, "Oh, thanks, Mr. Hyde," and handed him his card.

There were whispers between sips of hot chocolate as the crowd gathered behind the torches, and watched Vanessa take off her warm-up outfit. Underneath, she was wearing a sea-blue skating costume. She bent down, and tightened her laces, said something to the DJ, went onto the ice, and began to skate a warm-up lap around the perimeter of the pond.

"I think she likes you" Gina broke my staring.

"What?" I turned to her.

"I think she likes you. I saw her frown when she thought we were together."

"Do you mean it? 'Cause, I thought I saw that too,

but I wasn't sure if I was just imagining it." I turned to her excitedly. "No, it was a frown all right." Gina tapped me on the shoulder, "Quiet. She's about to begin." She pointed to Vanessa who was in a meditating stance on the other side of the pond. The unmistakable and beautiful voice of Enya entered the night.

Vanessa skated around the edge of the pond and approaching where her father was standing, twisted in the air while everyone clapped at her perfect landing. She continued in unison with Enya's voice and did another impressive spin on the other side of the pond. The dimly lit ice made her look more like an angel flying to heaven than a figure skater attempting a double lutz or whatever they call it. She picked up speed and headed toward the middle of the pond. From the music, everyone could sense a big jump ahead. Vanessa positioned herself to jump but no jump came. I couldn't believe what I was witnessing. No one could. It took a few seconds for everyone to comprehend what had happened. Her scream was what made me realize it was real. "Help!"

"Oh, my God!" someone yelled.

Vanessa had fallen through the ice!

"No!" Mr. Hyde yelled and ran across the ice, sliding and falling a couple of times.

"Someone stop him!" I hollered but no one listened. It was complete chaos. People were running around but no one knew what to do. I knew the worst thing was for Mr. Hyde to try to rescue Vanessa without the proper equipment. I was right. Seconds later, he had also fallen in the pond. I had to act quickly.

"Gina! Your truck!" That's all I had to say. Gina ran to her truck and I followed. I spotted the loose rope that designated the parking area, untied it, and jumped into Gina's truck. She put the truck into four-wheel drive and leaned on the horn while driving toward the pond.

She turned to me. "Let's hope this holds us."

Our minds were on the same page as she drove her truck onto the ice and went halfway out onto the pond before she parked.

"When I raise my hand, you back up," I said as I hopped out of the truck. I took the rope and began tying it to the front bumper.

"Help!" It was Mr. Hyde's voice.

"Hold on. I'll be right there!" I shouted back.

"It's Vanessa! She's swallowed a lot of water! Hurry!"

I tugged on the rope to see if it would hold. It did. I slid cautiously across the ice until I reached the edge of the hole. Mr. Hyde was holding onto Vanessa, and she didn't look conscious. My eyes bulged at the sight.

"Here!" I threw him the rope and he grabbed it and wrapped his arms under Vanessa while keeping her in front of him. I turned back to Gina's headlights and emphatically raised my arm. The engine roared and the tires squealed for a second. I prayed that the truck wouldn't fall through the ice. I knew Gina was probably doing the same thing because she didn't race, but slowly backed the truck up pulling Mr. Hyde and Vanessa closer to me. It was working. I heard the sound of a siren and glanced back and saw the lights of an ambulance flickering through the trees.

"Hold on, Mr. Hyde. You're almost there," I tried keep him alert. His face had a blank look.

"My little girl. My little girl. She can't breathe. little girl."

Oh, no, I'm losing him, I thought. "Mr. Hyde! He comes an ambulance. They're going to help her! Just few more feet."

There was suddenly a loud snap. The rope brok and they both went under for what seemed to be eternity but then resurfaced. I was standing inches aw Their only hope was for me to pull them out. I grabbe Mr. Hyde by the coat and I thought I was going to fall too. There was no way I was strong enough to pull the out. What am I going to do? I wondered.

The question was suddenly answered when anoth figure ran across the ice toward me. I recognized th bulky figure immediately—Dan "Franco" Francais. In ha a second, Franco's lineman's arms pulled Mr. Hyde ar Vanessa out of the water to safety. Seconds later, EM were sliding along the ice with stretchers, and before could even see how Mr. Hyde and Vanessa were doin the red and white lights faded into the night, and Enya voice had been replaced by the distant eerie siren.

CHAPTER SIX

THE BELLTOWN HOSPITAL was an absolute zoo. Everyone was trying to find out how Vanessa was doing. Word was out that Mr. Hyde was holding up except they were treating him for a slight case of shock. The question was Vanessa. No one knew. Or no one was talking. Rumors began flying. "I heard she's in a coma," said one person.

"I heard she's fine," answered another. Finally, Dr. Alden walked into the lobby to face the crowd.

"How is she?" someone shouted.

"Shut up, and let the man talk," yelled another voice in the crowd.

"No, it's OK. How is she, you ask? To be perfectly honest, it's too early to tell. Vanessa swallowed a lot of water and there were some other complications that I can't get into right now. I just wanted all of you to know

Dr. Richardson is doing his best."

"What kind of complications?" Gina asked, but Dr. Alden had already turned and headed through the swinging doors that lead to the emergency room. I guess because everyone was talking to each other no one noticed me follow him or if they did they didn't care. I knew I was breaking the rules. But, I really didn't care about getting into trouble. All I cared about was finding some answers. I spotted two nurses coming in my direction, approaching Dr. Alden. I ducked into a door-way and listened.

"Doctor, do you think the Hyde girl will make it?" I heard one ask.

"I think so, but we still have an unexplained case of acidosis on our hands," he said.

"I wonder what caused it?" he asked.

"We'll know in a couple of minutes. Dr. Richardson is running some tests."

Dr. Alden went on his way but the nurses were still standing outside the door, chatting. Then they left too.

I opened the door and slipped along the wall but stopped when I saw Dr. Alden talking with Dr. Richardson. I got within earshot and took refuge behind a crash cart.

"Are you sure?" Dr. Alden asked.

"I'm positive. The tests revealed that the girl had toxic doses of ethylene glycol in her body."

"My God, why would she have that in her system?" Dr. Alden asked.

"I was hoping you could tell me. You're her doctor. Has she ever been suicidal or had to see a psychiatrist?"

"Not to my knowledge. She seems to be a well-adjusted kid. But, if I'm wrong we can deal with that later. Is she going to be OK?" Dr. Alden asked.

I leaned over in anticipation of Dr. Richardson's answer.

"Yes, I treated her with..." He didn't finish because he was watching me fall to the floor.

"Hey, what are you doing in here?" Dr. Richardson snapped.

"Sorry," I gave a weak apology.

"Orville, you know you're not supposed to be in here." Dr. Alden recognized me.

"I'm sorry, but I had to find out how Vanessa was doing."

"She's going to be fine, son. I'll be right out to tell everyone. Don't say anything because it's best if I fill the people in. OK?" Dr. Alden had an understanding look.

I was tempted to ask the question What does suicidal have to do with falling through the ice? But I just nodded my head yes and turned in the other direction. I didn't want to ruffle any feathers. After all, the most important question had been answered; Vanessa was going to live! I do have to admit, though, when I got back into the lobby the phrase toxic doses of ethylene glycol made me wonder what it was and why was it in Vanessa Hyde's system. I took some change out of my jeans' pocket and headed to the pay phone—I had to find out.

I hung the phone up in frustration. Mrs. Wilder had just informed me that Dr. Wilder was playing hoops in the over-thirty league at the Belltown Recreation De-

partment. That explained why I hadn't seem him at P
grim Pond supporting Douglas Hyde.

"Ethylene glycol," I whispered to myself so
wouldn't forget the name. God knows, if it had bee
mentioned in my biology class it would've already bee
out of my head. I walked over to Gina and Franco wh
were talking to the nosy reporter.

"I mean, they're saying the reason the ice broke w
possibly because of an under-water spring. So, how d
you know your truck wouldn't fall through the ice?" I
put pen to pad.

"I didn't know. It was just an impulsive thing to d
We were lucky I guess. But, sir, with all due respect
don't think we should be talking about that right no
Let's worry about Vanessa," Gina said.

The reporter reluctantly put away his pen and pa
I knew now was my chance to ask the reporter a que
tion that had been bothering me.

"Excuse me, but I'm into journalism, and I was r
ally interested in the questions you asked Mr. Hyde ea
lier. Could I ask you a few questions?" Even though
thought he was annoying I figured I'd give him a co
pliment and some attention and I would get some a
swers. Gina and Franco looked at me like I was a litt
crazy while the reporter looked psyched that anyo
had paid him any mind.

"Sure. Fire away." He smiled patronizingly.

"Well, it seems the only issue you asked about w
Fisherman's Banks."

"If you excuse the pun, that's my only hook for

story. That's really the only issue where the candidates differ. The environmentalists are backing Hyde. The fishermen are backing Barry Field. I mean, the fishermen hate Douglas Hyde. But, who's to blame them, it's their livelihood. In fact, I've heard some of them say that they would rather see him dead."

My mind was clicking but I continued asking questions." Do you really think that if Douglas Hyde were elected, he would get a bill passed to close the Banks for six years?"

The guy laughed. "Now who's the reporter? I really don't know, but if your life was fishing in those banks would you want to take the chance of finding out how much power Douglas Hyde has in the Congress? No way. You'd back Barry Field to the end. You'd vote for him."

"And threaten Douglas Hyde," I softly whispered as a smiling Dr. Alden appeared through the swinging doors.

Gina, Franco, and I squeezed into Gina's truck. We were pretty drained from the near tragedy, but certainly relieved. Vanessa was doing fine. She would have to stay overnight for observation. Mr. Hyde was also doing well. I figured he probably came out of it when he saw Vanessa was all right. Gina dropped Franco off at his house, but before he got out I asked,

"Franco, how did you end up at Pilgrim Pond anyway?"

"Oh, I went to your house to see if you wanted to

hang out and your mom told me you went to Pilgr
Pond and there was going to be all sorts of food so-
Franco stopped. Gina and I had interrupted him w
our laughter.

"Hey, you guys, if we want to win the division ne
year..."

"I'm going to need to put some meat on my bone
Gina and I finished his sentence in unison. Fran
couldn't help but laugh.

"I guess I've used that one too much."

"In all seriousness, Vanessa might not be alive if y
didn't have the craving for food," I said.

"Orville, don't give me all the credit. It was all of
Three teenage kids saving the day as the adults i
around like chickens with their heads cut off. See y
later." Franco shut the door behind him.

"Later," Gina and I both answered.

"So, you want me to drop you off?" Gina aske
think she knew something was on my mind.

"Nah, can we go to the rec center?"

"The rec center? Does this have something to
with the case?"

"Why?" I asked.

"Because, Officer Jameson is tailing us and I'll lc
him again. Just say the word," Gina said excitedly. I kn
she wanted me to say lose him, but I didn't.

"It could have something to do with the case, b
you don't have to lose him. After all, if he hadn't follow
us to Pilgrim Pond the ambulance wouldn't have gott
there so quickly. He's the one who called it in," I said, b

in my mind I was saying something else—Ethylene glycol. What did it mean?

While we watched the last three minutes of the basketball game, I told Gina what I had heard in the emergency room and prepped her on how we should ask Dr. Wilder about ethylene glycol. Gina didn't need much prepping, she was the queen of playing along. Speaking of playing, I couldn't believe how good Dr. Wilder was at hoops. In the three minutes we watched, he hit two three-pointers, had a steal, and even got off his feet to reject a shot. His team won by twelve points. He walked off the court out of breath and I threw him a towel.

"And you said there was only one doctor who could operate." I smiled.

Dr. Wilder caught the towel and smiled back, "Not bad for an older man." He toweled off.

"I was just thinking the same thing except the phrase I was thinking was 'not bad for an old man.' You're almost as good as my dad."

"Orville, that really hurts. I put him to shame last year. Why do you think he picked the two months of rec basketball season to teach over in Ireland? He doesn't want to face me." He laughed and then realized Gina was with me. "Oh, hi, Gina, how are you doing?"

"Great, Dr. Wilder."

"Dave," he stressed.

"Dave," Gina smiled.

"I could be vain enough to think you guys car here to learn by watching an artist perfecting his cra but something tells me that you're here for somethi else. Actually, I called my wife at half-time and she sa you called me."

"Yes, I actually called for Gina."

"OK." Dr. Wilder sat on the bleachers beside us.

"Yes, you see Orville was telling me how you help him on a U.S. history paper." Gina waited for Dr. Wilde response.

"Yes, but I'd hardly say that I helped him. I gave hi a few tidbits of information about Doug Hyde." I stopped for a second. "Oh no, that reminds me—Do was going to have a fund-raiser tonight at Pilgrim Por I forgot all about it."

There was a sense of uneasiness, but we still didi say anything.

"Anyway, I was wondering if I could pick your bra for a paper I'm working on for my science class," Gi said.

"Yeah, no problem. If I can't answer it I shouldi have a job at Belltown Oceanographic."

"Is ethylene gly..." she forgot how to pronounce and looked at me for help.

"Glycol." I nodded for her to continue.

"Yes, is ethylene glycol lethal?"

"It is if you swallow enough of it—it will kill you. fact, sometimes suicidal people use it because it's accessible."

"What do you mean accessible?"

"I suppose there are many things that could kill you that are accessible, but ethylene glycol is a main ingredient in antifreeze. Swallow a jug of that and that's the show."

"Antifreeze!" The words blurted out of my mouth at the vision of Douglas Hyde when he found the three empty jugs of antifreeze.

"That's what I said, Orville, antifreeze."

I took over the questioning. "Dr. Wilder, if someone poured antifreeze on ice, would the ice melt?"

"I don't know why you would want to use antifreeze to melt ice." He looked at me.

"Hypothetically?" I pushed.

"Yes, of course, it's antifreeze. So, if you pour enough of it on, it would eat right through the ice."

"Oh, my God!" Gina and I both said.

"What's this all about?" Dr. Wilder frowned.

"Nothing, really," I said. I knew it was lame acting.

"Dr. Wilder, antifreeze has that green color so wouldn't that color be all over the ice?" Gina asked.

Hmmm, I thought, good point, Gina.

"That's true, if you used a certain brand, but the coloring is just an additive. I have seen some no-name brands that don't use the additive and are almost as clear as water."

No-name brands. That's the clincher, I thought. The empty jugs were no-name brands.

"I'm really confused, I thought this had to do with your science paper, Gina. This doesn't make sense. What's the topic?" Dr. Wilder wanted some answers.

"Yes, well..." Gina looked at me. I didn't know what to say to help her.

"Well, you see..." Gina didn't finish because Mrs. Wilder walked briskly toward us with a worried look.

"Honey, is something wrong?" Dr. Wilder asked, knowing the look.

"Dana Yoerger from the Oceanographic called. Vanessa Hyde's in the hospital."

"What? Is she OK?" Dr. Wilder shot up out of the bleacher seat.

"Yes, I'll tell you all about it in the car." She turned and walked out the door. She was too upset to greet us.

"If you two will excuse me," Dr. Wilder hurried after her.

After they were out of view Gina said, "We probably should have told him."

"Yeah, but he'll put it all together soon enough." I nodded.

"Now what?" Gina asked.

"Somehow, we're going to have to let Douglas Hyde know that it was no accident that Vanessa fell through the ice. Someone was definitely trying to kill her."

I picked up a stray basketball and contemplated taking a shot, but then dropped it to the floor realizing there was no more time for playing games.

After much thought, Gina and I went to the police station, and found Shane. We told him our theory of how the ice melted, but we left out all the other information about the threats, so his eyebrows raised with a you-gotta-be-kidding me look.

"Mr. Hyde might have some valid information that would make it easier for you to believe that someone deliberately melted the ice," that's all I said. I still considered the Hydes my clients and I wasn't going to compromise my obligation to keep silent about their affairs, at least not completely! I wrote a quick note to Mr. Hyde to call me, and gave it to Shane to give to him. Shane agreed and then said, "I still have no leads on who forced you into the harbor."

I gave an indifferent shrug. Something told me by including him, I had just given him his first lead.

I lay in my bed tossing and turning, thinking about the near tragedy, the threats to expose Mr. Hyde's past, and the reporter saying the fishermen would rather see Mr. Hyde dead than be elected to Congress. How did they all connect? Maybe, they didn't connect at all and I was forcing a pattern. Of course, I didn't know what that pattern was. I turned over again and thanked God that Vanessa was all right.

"After all," I said softly, "it would have been horrible if Mr. Hyde lost another daughter to drowning, and this time he would've witnessed it. Thank God, he didn't go into complete shock."

Then it dawned on me—whoever put the antifreeze on the ice may not have been trying to kill Vanessa at all. After all, they knew there would be a big crowd watching so there was always a chance that she'd be rescued. No, I thought, they figured on something far more beneficial to their plans. They figured Douglas Hyde would lose it completely watching his daughter drown, and end up in a mental hospital again. He proved them wrong by going after his daughter. Sure, he was shaken after the event, but that's natural especially for someone who had experienced two horrific tragedies. He was stronger than they or he or she anticipated. Whoever this person or people were, they liked playing mind games, and ironically, I felt that was the key—Douglas Hyde's mind. I turned over and was about to fall asleep when the phone rang. I eased out of bed and grabbed the phone on the third ring.

"Hello," I yawned.

"Orville, Doug Hyde. Sorry if I woke you."

"No problem."

"It's just that I need to talk to you."

"That makes two of us," I said while rubbing my eyes awake.

CHAPTER
SEVEN

ON ANY OTHER Sunday morning there was no way I'd be up at seven. Nine tops. Seven in the morning? No way! But, this wasn't any other Sunday morning to me. This was the first day in my short career as an investigator that an adult really felt I could help. The previous night Douglas Hyde and I talked for twenty minutes about a number of things: how I figured out the ice was deliberately melted; how Hyde informed Shane about the threats; what to do now?

He told me, "Detective O'Connell is going to have one of his informants ask around the harbors throughout the Cape to see if any of the fishermen have mentioned 'taking care of me.' He thinks it all might have something to do with my stand on closing the Banks. He said his man will be discreet, but, at this point, I don't care about that. All I care about is my daughter's safety."

"I'm glad Shane is looking at that angle because I think it has something to do with the Banks, but there are still some things nagging at me," I said.

"What are they?"

"The flattened penny, the lavender material from the very same dress that Theresa Bigelow wore, and the fact that someone tried to drive you crazy by making you watch your daughter almost drown. Mr. Hyde, when is your next appointment with the hypnotist?"

"Tuesday. 10:00 AM. Why?"

"Can you push it up to tomorrow?"

"Tomorrow's Sunday."

"I know but we might not have till Tuesday. For some crazy reason, I think your appointment with the hypnotist could be a key to all of this."

"I'll call you back in five minutes." He hung up.

A few minutes later the phone rang.

Hyde skipped the greeting, "I'm meeting her at 7:30 tomorrow morning."

"Good, I want to come," I said.

"I don't know."

"Look"—I was firm—"I want to make sure all the right questions are asked and answered."

There was silence on the other end for a long time and finally,

"There's no use fighting you, Orville. I might as well face it, you might be a teenager but you sure know what you're doing. I'll pick you up at 7:00 and I'll bring some coffee and doughnuts and explain the whole process."

The late hour brought validation and then sleep, but now it was Sunday morning at 7:00 AM, and I was praying the early hour would bring Mr. Hyde with some coffee to wake me. It did. We parked by Cranberry Beach and he told me he called the hypnotist and asked if I could sit in.

"She told me that if you have any questions during the procedure to write them on a piece of paper and she'll ask me. She also wanted you to know the two other times that I was under, I talked like an eight-year-old so don't be surprised."

"What do you mean talked like an eight-year-old?"

"Since I'm reliving a scene from when I was eight, I might talk and have mannerisms of a boy that age. She was worried that you might laugh, and that would be distracting."

"This is no laughing matter," I said, and threw my last piece of doughnut out the window and watched two seagulls swoop down out of nowhere and gobble it up.

"Beautiful creatures, aren't they? It's strange, isn't it, how there'll be no seagulls in sight and the moment you throw a piece of food on the ground they appear like they have been watching from heaven above."

"I think they have," I said before Mr. Hyde started the engine and pulled out of Cranberry Beach.

I wish I could describe how the hypnotist, Dr. Higgins, put Mr. Hyde under hypnosis, but I can't. She was very clear that I couldn't come into the room until Mr. Hyde was in the trance or whatever they call it. She told me that her methods may be different from most hypnotists, but nonetheless, they were successful, and that's all that mattered. I agreed. I waited outside her office for about ten minutes, doodling with the pen and pad she had provided for questions. Finally, just when I figured she may have changed her mind and wasn't going to let me sit in, her office door slowly opened. She waved me in, pointed to a chair, and then made a shush sign with her finger to her mouth. I nodded and took my seat. She sat back down and turned to Mr. Hyde who was sitting cross-legged on the floor with his eyes closed.

"OK, Doug, we've had a lot of fun talking about your friend Theresa, haven't we?"

"Yes, Theresa's my best buddy."

It was true. He did sound like a little kid. Or maybe more like an adult impersonating a little kid.

"Can we talk more about Theresa and things you two do?"

"Sure."

"Do you like Theresa?"

"Well, yeah, for a girl and all. If we have to get married we're going to marry each other." He fidgeted with his hands.

I was glad I had been warned about the child's voice and mannerisms. I don't know if I would have laughed, it was more eerie than anything, but I certainly would have had some sort of reaction.

"If you have to, you'll marry Theresa when you get older. When did you two decide this?" Her voice was soft.

"In the park. I got these sparklers for my birthday and I gave Theresa one and asked her to marry me."

"Yes, you told me about the park the last time we talked. Now let's talk about another day with Theresa."

"OK."

"Tell me about her birthday May 4, 1962."

His eyes stayed shut but he moved around a little.

"It's OK, Doug, we can talk about the beginning of the day. Are you going to Theresa's party?"

"Sort of, but I'm not invited."

I noticed how Dr. Higgins asked the question in the present tense, and that's how Mr. Hyde answered it. I knew that in his mind it was May 4, 1962.

"Why aren't you invited?"

"'Cause, Mr. Bigelow is a jerk. He doesn't like me because my parents aren't rich like him. But, Theresa told me he's not rich anymore."

"OK. But, you say that you're going to the party anyway. Now, Doug, think real hard, OK?"

Mr. Hyde nodded.

"Good. You're at the party."

"Not really. I'm hiding in the bushes. Theresa's talking to some girls." He began to laugh.

"What's so funny, Doug?"

"Theresa just made a face behind Annie Melden's back. She hates her."

"So is Theresa having fun?"

"No way."

"Why not?"

"'Cause, I'm not there."

I almost wanted to laugh at how confident he was with girls at age eight.

"Are you going to join the party?"

"No, it's just for girls. It's stupid anyway."

"Are you going to hide in the bushes all night?"

"No, I'm going to try to get Theresa's attention."

"How are you going to do that?"

"I got all these pennies. I'll throw one at her."

I wrote on the pad and raised it so Dr. Higgins could read it. She nodded and asked, "Before you throw the penny, tell me what Theresa is wearing?"

"Oh, it's some fancy dress her father gave her yesterday."

I wrote again and Dr. Higgins asked, "Is the color lavender?"

"Yeah, that's what she told me yesterday. But, I told her that's just a fancy name for light purple."

"What kind of shoes is she wearing?"

"They're lady's shoes—white ones—like the kind my mother wears to important stuff. She looks tall in them."

High heels, I thought.

"OK, Doug. You threw the penny and did it hit her?" He laughed.

"Yup, right in the head. She's looking over at the bushes." He made a weird sound.

"What's that?"

"That's a bird call. She's laughing at how bad it was. She's looking around making sure no one sees her."

"Does she come to the bushes?"

"Yup. She sneaks into the bushes and says, 'Shush, let's go have some fun,' and she shows me the penny I threw at her."

"What do you do then?"

"I light my last two sparklers left over from my birthday and I give her one."

Dr. Higgins glanced over at me like you better hold on, here comes the tough part. Almost everything I had heard so far, Mr. Hyde had already told me so I was still a little skeptical about the whole thing.

"Doug, do you stay in the bushes?"

"No, we head for the train tracks, but we go to the park first."

"Now, Doug, I want you to think hard. I want you to go to the train tracks."

I could see the concentration in Mr. Hyde's face as he sifted the information that was in his brain.

Finally, he said, "OK."

"What are you doing at the train tracks?"

"We put pennies on the tracks. We do that all the time."

"Where is Theresa when you put the pennies on the tracks?"

"She's right beside me." He began laughing.

"What's so funny?"

"Theresa says the next train that comes we should

jump on and go to Boston and see the Red Sox. She likes Carl Yastrzemski. I think he he has a big fat nose."

Mr. Hyde then moved his head a little.

"What do you see, Doug?"

"Lights. There's a train coming. It's not that far away."

"So are you going to get off the tracks?"

"Oh, yeah, I just did. I'm running behind the bushes. I am looking back and Theresa is still on the tracks."

"What's she doing?"

"Her foot is stuck or something. I'm scared."

"What are you doing?" Dr. Higgins and I both felt the tension.

"I am running toward her and ... and ... she throws her shoe at me."

"Why?"

A smile appeared on his face, "She was kidding. Her foot's not stuck at all." He laughed again.

"What's so funny?"

"She shouted at me, "'Fraidy cat, 'fraidy cat, steal a Yankee's basseball bat.'"

"So, she is OK?" Dr. Higgins asked surprised.

"Yeah, she was just joking."

"How far away is the train?"

"About a football field away." A hundred yards, I thought.

"Is Theresa looking at the train?"

"Yes, she's going to cross the tracks." His head shook again.

"What do you see, Doug?"

"I thought I saw a shadow behind her."

He shook again.

"What is it?"

"I think it's a man coming out of the woods. I can't tell. He's grabbing her. 'Theresa watch out!'"

He shook like he was having a convulsion, and his eyelids opened for a brief second before they shut again.

"What, Doug? What is it?"

"A smell. There's a really bad smell."

"Where's Theresa?"

"I don't know. I don't ... I can't see. It's getting foggy. I feel like I can't breathe. The smell is horrible."

"Do you see anything?"

"White. A white cloth," He was fading off a bit and I thought he was going to pass out. "Yes, a white cloth. It's on my nose and mouth. The taste is terrible. I can't breathe. I can't…"

Dr. Higgins looked over at me and shook her head, "OK, Doug, that's fine. That's enough for now. I'm going to count to three and when you wake, you will not remember the feeling you have right now, and you won't remember what you told me. One. Two. Three."

Mr. Hyde woke up and stared at Dr. Higgins and then at me.

"Well, did I just stand there and watch Theresa get hit by the train?"

No, but someone else watched, I thought and turned to Dr. Higgins as she began to fill him in.

I figured I should give Mr. Hyde a few minutes to digest the startling information of May 4, 1962, before I bombarded him with questions. His mind must have been spinning with thoughts as he drove me home. I know my mind was. I didn't have to speculate about the white cloth and the terrible smell. The same thing had happened to me during a case once and Mr. Hyde's description brought it all back. I was positive someone had put drugs on a cloth and forced the eight-year-old Doug Hyde to inhale fumes until he passed out. I waited until we were about five minutes from my house when I couldn't resist anymore.

"Mr. Hyde, I've been thinking."

"You're not the only one," he sighed.

"You must have been treated after the accident. Did the doctor consider that maybe you were drugged?"

"I would've remembered that. And ... I don't."

"Who was the doctor that treated you?"

"I really don't remember. You see for two weeks after the accident, I was kind of out of it. From the shock of it all, I was probably on medication."

"You don't remember the doctor at all?"

"Well. Let's see. I think it could been Dr. Alden. He was our family doctor."

"Dr. Alden? He was a doctor back in 1962?"

"Yes, he was just starting out." He stopped. "Yes, I think it could've been Dr. Alden."

I tried not to react but continued my questioning.

"There are a couple of other things that are bothering me."

"Go right ahead."

"Whoever is doing all of this knows that you were in a mental hospital, so why didn't they just leak that to the press instead? I mean, no offense, but you talk about speculation being dangerous. If people knew that, your chances would be hurt severely."

"Yes, you're right, but they wouldn't have the proof. The place I went to is a private institution in Maine, and they don't keep records exclusively for that reason. If I didn't want my stay there to come out, it wouldn't."

"Have you told anyone about your stay there?"

"Just you the other day and..." He paused for a second and then the words fell from his mouth, "Dr. Alden."

He pulled over to the side of the road and parked.

"Don't even think it, Orville. Dr. Alden is like a father to me."

"Hear me out, Mr. Hyde. You say Dr. Alden treated you."

"I'm not positive," he jumped in.

"Well, we can find that out easily enough. You also said that he was the only person you told about your stay in a private hospital in Maine, a hospital that doesn't keep records. Wow."

The thought popped into my head. "And finally, the person who sent you a piece of Theresa's dress would've had access to the train accident scene. Who wouldn't have had better access to an accident scene than a doctor!"

Mr. Hyde's face turned pale and he was silent for a minute.

"What would Dr. Alden have against me? Why would he do this to me?"

"That's the only part that doesn't seem to fit. There doesn't seem to be a motive."

I had to admit that before I continued. "But, even as we speak there are a couple of other things that point to him like who else would have access to drugs. And who would think about messing with your mental state like forcing you to watch another daughter drown but a doctor."

"You make good points but...but...Dr. Alden is my friend." Mr. Hyde wasn't buying it.

"Can you think of any motive at all? You can be as farfetched as you want."

"Dr. Alden was good friends with Theresa's father."

"No, that wouldn't work because Mr. Bigelow wouldn't have anything against you until after the accident. If what I'm suggesting is true, Dr. Alden was responsible for the accident. But, that reminds me of my other question, whatever happened to Mr. Bigelow?"

"After Theresa was buried, he moved out of Belltown."

"Did he blame you for her death because you brought her to the train tracks?"

"Yes, the night after she was buried, Bigelow came to our house. I don't remember any of it, because I was sedated, but they told me that he was drunk and threw a bottle at my house and cursed my family. The strangest thing, though ... about a month later I received a letter from him saying it wasn't my fault about Theresa. I still read it now and then to convince myself. After today's session, I might not have to read it anymore." Mr. Hyde put the car in drive and pulled onto the road.

"So, you still have the letter?"

"Yes.

"I would like to see it."

"OK." He parked in front of my house.

"I know you have to pick Vanessa up from the hospital. So, why don't I stop by your house in two hours."

"Sure. What about your Dr. Alden theory?"

"I'll notify Shane. We need more to go on than just my hunches. They could be just crazy thoughts," I said, knowing that Mr. Hyde might bump into Dr. Alden in the hospital. Even though he didn't seem to put much stock in my theory, I still didn't want him doing anything rash. I didn't want to jump the gun either. There were still some points that didn't seem to jell about Dr. Alden.

One, he was one of the most cherished people in Belltown. Two, he seemed *totally* concerned about Vanessa in the emergency room, and the third and most important point that didn't make sense—*motive*. He didn't have one or did he?

CHAPTER EIGHT

I sat in Mr. Hyde's study and read the letter from Theresa Bigelow's father for the third time.

June 2, 1962
Dear Doug,
I am writing to apologize for blaming you for my little Theresa's death. I now know it was an accident. It wasn't your fault. I am sorry that I blamed you, and I don't want you to live with this tragedy on your hands. She is in a far better place now.
Sincerely,
Jordan Bigelow

I looked at the front of the envelope—no return address, but it was postmarked: Case City, West Virginia. "Bizarre," I said to Mr. Hyde, and handed him the letter.

"What do you mean, bizarre?"

"Well, first of all the fact that he forgives you. I mean, it was a month later."

"Yes, but what's so bizarre about that?"

"I just think that it's strange that you say he never liked you and that he blamed you for her death and then, less than a month later, he sent you a letter of forgiveness. But, the really bizarre part is"—I paused and motioned for the letter and scanned for the line— "I *now* know it was an accident. I *now* know it was an accident. Didn't he know it was an accident the night it happened?" I handed back the letter. Mr. Hyde looked down at it for a second before placing it back into the envelope.

"I always took that line to mean he *now* accepted it in his mind as an accident. You know with the rumors and all."

"That's true, I didn't think of it that way," I admitted. Mr. Hyde nodded and opened his desk and put the letter away.

"Mr. Hyde, did Jordan Bigelow have relatives in Case City, Virginia?"

"Not that I know of. All of his people were from Lowell, Massachusetts."

"So why did he end up moving there?"

"Probably to get as far away from Belltown as possible. You have to remember, Orville, his wife had died from a fall the previous year."

"Yes, tell me again how that happened?"

"Mrs. Bigelow was walking around Belltown Heights Hill and it was a foggy night and she just lost her footing and … I really don't see the relevance."

"I don't either. I was just curious." I had to admit again.

The phone rang and Hyde answered it.

I thought to myself, the letter could have been just one of sympathy to Douglas Hyde, so he wouldn't carry the burden of Theresa Bigelow's death on his shoulders. But, it just seemed to go against Jordan Bigelow's character to write a letter of that nature. Of course, I really was going by the few details that Mr. Hyde could remember about the man—a man who didn't like him and blamed him for his daughter's death. I had to find out more about that night.

"Orville?" Mr. Hyde brought me out of my trance.

"Oh, I'm sorry. Was that Shane or somebody connected with the case?"

"No, it was just some folks down at Town Hall asking how Vanessa was feeling."

"It's Sunday. Isn't Town Hall closed?"

"No, since it's being renovated, they're on a really crazy work schedule."

"Oh." I paused in thought. "Wait a minute. The Town Hall is open today?"

"Yes, till 5:00."

"Perfect," I murmured to myself.

Before I headed for Town Hall, I checked on Vanessa, who was sound asleep. I decided since Officer Jameson was still following me in the beat-up old Buick and I was on foot, I might as well hitch a ride. He didn't seem to mind. I think he was relieved to know exactly where I was going. I gave him some excuse about paying the excise tax for my mom, but there was a far greater reason for my trip. I wanted to get Theresa Bigelow's death certificate, and check out the name of the doctor who had signed it. I wondered if it would be Dr. Alden. If it was Alden, that would make the finger of guilt easier to point. But, there still wouldn't be motives for him to kill Theresa Bigelow and then to use that event, almost four decades later, to blackmail Mr. Hyde not to run for Congress. I mean, Dr. Alden is a doctor not a fisherman. By far, this was my most confusing case, I thought as I approached the town clerk's office. There was a well-dressed, elderly woman standing behind the counter.

She smiled and raised her hand, "Wait..."

I stopped in my tracks.

"You're a Jacques aren't you?"

I was taken a little off guard, "Ahh ... Orville Jacques, but how did you know?"

"You're the spitting image of your father."

"Well, that explains my lack of social life."

The woman giggled, "Oh, and you have his sense of humor too."

I thought, Uh oh, no kid ever wants to have the same sense of humor as his parents.

"How do you know my dad?"

"I took his English class at the adult school. He was always so wonderful to volunteer his time. If I were thirty years ... a little younger your mother would be in trouble." She laughed.

"Now what can I do for you, Orville?"

"Well, I was..." I stopped. "I didn't catch your name."

"My name is Jan Murray but everyone calls me Sunny."

"How appropriate."

"Oh, you're such a charmer." She blushed.

"Well, Sunny, I was wondering if you could find me this death certificate?" I handed her the piece of paper on which I had scribbled the name and date.

She peered down and back up at me. "I remember this. Theresa Bigelow. She was hit by a train the day of her birthday."

"Yes."

"It was tragic. Let me find it for you." Sunny suddenly didn't seem so sunny. I watched her go into the back and search through a couple of file cabinets for about five minutes before she returned. "I'm sorry, I can't find it."

"You mean it's missing!" I said.

"Well, temporarily. You see, with all the renovations going on most of the old birth and death certificates are in storage so that's probably where it is. Bonnie O'Neil who works here full-time would be able to track it down for you if you come back tomorrow. I just volunteer. It gives me something to do."

"Thanks, I might do that." I tried to hide my frustration.

Sunny sighed. "I still say a prayer for that little girl— to die on your birthday, terrible, terrible."

"Yeah, and her poor father every year has to be reminded it was the anniversary of his daughter's death."

"Poor father?" Sunny gave me a questioning stare.

"Yes. Why not?" I asked.

She pointed a finger for me to move closer as she leaned on the counter, "You never heard the rumor?"

"No, what rumor?" I rested my elbows on the counter.

"Well, this is an old Belltown rumor. About two weeks after little Theresa died, her father moved out of Belltown. He had his lawyer sell his house and his clothing factory in Lowell." Sunny paused and looked around. She was enjoying the fact that I was hanging on every word.

"So he couldn't deal with his daughter's death and got rid of everything. What's so strange about that?" I asked.

"About a month or so later his lawyer, Willard Shelton, was in a bar. He got to drinking—he had a real problem with alcohol—So anyway, some people got to talking about poor Jordan Bigelow and how he lost his wife and now his little daughter and his business and all. But, Willard Shelton said..." Sunny stopped again and looked around.

"What?" The suspense was killing me.

"'Don't worry about Jordan Bigelow, he had life insurance policies on both his wife and little girl.' Everyone said he must have been kidding. But Shelton insisted. 'Kidding? I did all the legal work for him. Three hundred thousand dollars a person.'"

I was dizzy and my mind was racing with thoughts. I had to get out of Town Hall and fit this major piece into my puzzle.

"Orville, are you OK?"

"Yes, Sunny. Where can I find this Willard Shelton?"

"I really couldn't tell you. He lost his license to practice law. He opened his mouth about his clients once too often. Someone told me he started his own business or something, but for the life of me, I don't remember what it was."

"Well, thanks a lot, Sunny."

"I wish I could've been more help."

"Believe me, Sunny, you were. You were!"

It was only 2:00 in the afternoon, but I decided to lie down on my bed and try to clear my head. I thought my head was going to explode from all the questions that were pounding away. Was Jordan Bigelow capable of pushing his own daughter in front of a train? Could money drive someone to commit a crime like that? If money was this man's god, why would he then sell his business? If he was that greedy for wealth wouldn't he expand the business? Also, if wealth was his concern, why would he move to a small place like Case City, West Virginia? And why would he send that letter to Doug Hyde? And why didn't Doug Hyde mention the rumor? Actually, that question was easy to answer—since he was involved in the tragedy, people probably never talked about the rumor in front of him or anything else dealing with the accident.

And then there was the question of an accomplice.

If what Hyde remembered under hypnosis was true, at least two people had to be involved. One, to grab Theresa, the other, to grab Doug Hyde. All the questions about Dr. Alden were still there plus the added fact that Mr. Hyde had told me—Mr. Bigelow and Dr. Alden were friends. But still none of this explained why Hyde was being blackmailed. I mean, if Jordan Bigelow and Dr. Alden committed the crime and got away with it, wouldn't they want to keep it quiet? Why ... My millionth "why" was interrupted by the ringing phone.

"Orville, Shane here."

"Shane, what's up?"

"I thought you might like to know that we're questioning someone about the Hyde blackmail case."

"Who is it?" My voice jumped.

"A fisherman named Patrick Belavance."

"Patrick Belavance?"

"The other night in front of people, he said he'd like to kill Hyde for what he's wants to do with Fisherman's Banks."

"Yeah, but a lot of fishermen have said that. That doesn't mean they actually will."

"But, do a lot of fisherman drive a truck with a snowplow? And do a lot of fishermen have six empty jugs of antifreeze in the back of their truck?"

"Wow." I was in shock.

"Plus we found cut-up magazines on his boat."

"Used for the threatening letters." I finished his sentence.

"You got it."

"But how does that tie this Belavance guy in with the lavender material, the flattened penny, and all that?"

"There were also some old newspaper articles about Theresa Bigelow's death in a trash can on the boat. Belavance must've heard about the Bigelow accident and how Hyde was involved and looked it up and used it to blackmail him. Of course, he's denying everything. Good actor. But, he'll talk soon enough. I just thought you'd like to be the first to know, and now you won't have to worry about Officer Jameson following you around. We killed two birds with one stone in this one."

"Thanks, Shane, but that still doesn't explain..."

"Orville, I really gotta get going. Hey, good work. See ya."

Click—gone.

All the information Shane provided seemed plausible, but there was something Shane overlooked—the lavender material came from the actual dress. How could Patrick Belavance, the fisherman, get a piece of material from the actual dress? Shane probably had a possible theory for that, and I forgave him for jumping the gun because I had information he didn't have. I had been at the hypnotist's office when Douglas Hyde revealed Theresa Bigelow's accident was no accident. In my heart, I knew that the killer of Theresa Bigelow and the blackmailer of Douglas Hyde had set Patrick Belavance up.

Earlier in the day, I had told Mr. Hyde I'd inform Shane of the details of the hypnotist's meeting, and I probably should've called Shane so he would stop interrogating Belavance. But, I also knew as long as Shane was questioning the fisherman, I had the upper hand on the killer. This way, I could continue snooping around, and I didn't have Officer Jameson following me. I was on the right path. I just had to go further.

As I grabbed my winter coat, I knew I had to stop speculating on who the killer/blackmailer was, and just let fate lead me to the guilty party. Or parties?

"Dr. Alden is with a patient. He said if you could go down to the cafeteria, he'll meet you there in about ten minutes. He's been here all night with two of his patients," said the nurse behind the counter.

"Oh, really?"

"Yes, a girl who fell through the ice and then another patient who had a stroke. Stayed right by them the whole time. He's a wonderful doctor." She smiled and went back to her paperwork as my stomach twisted in knots. It just didn't make sense that a caring man like Dr. Alden would be involved. Maybe, I was wrong about my doctor hunch. I knew in ten minutes I would know one way or the other. Well, anyway, I had ten minutes, so I figured I'd give Gina a call and put her to work.

"Gina?"

"Yeah, Orville."

"Yeah, I tried you earlier but I got the machine. Where were you?"

"I was here. I was on the other line. What's your problem?"

She sensed the edginess in my voice.

"Sorry, I'm just a little anxious. I think I'm getting closer with the Hyde case, but I need your help."

"Yeah, no problem. I got a pen, so fire away."

"Could you find out if Jordan Bigelow of Case City, West Virginia, is still alive? And if he is, could you find out his home phone number, address, and all that?"

"Sure, Orville. It might take a little while. Should I call you at The Shack?"

"No, I'll call you. Thanks, G." I hung up before her questions flew.

I was a bundle of nerves as I sipped on a soda in the cafeteria and waited for Dr. Alden. How should I approach him? I wondered. Do I beat around the bush, or do I go straight for the jugular and accuse him? I remembered how I falsely accused someone once and the result was painful, so I figured I'd calmly ask questions about May 4, 1962 and take it from there.

"Orville, how are you doing?" Dr. Alden sat across from me clutching a cup of coffee.

He looked tired and worn.

"Good, Dr. Alden." I forced a smile.

"It's great about Vanessa, huh?"

"Yes, sir."

"So, what can I do for you?" He leaned back in his chair and took a healthy swallow.

"Well…" I gulped. "I'm actually here to ask you about

the Hydes. How long have you been their family doctor?"

"Almost forty years. Ever since Doug was a little guy. But, I'm retiring at the end of this year. I'm going to hit every golf course around the world." He gave a light laugh and smiled.

I ignored the smile, "So, you were Mr. Hyde's doctor the night of Theresa Bigelow's accident?"

The smile vanished. "What's this all about, Orville?"

"Did you treat Doug Hyde the night of the accident?"

"Why are you asking me these questions? You're not going to uncover Doug's past are you? He doesn't need that brought up during his run for Congress."

"So, you care about his run for Congress?"

"Of course, I do. What kind of question is that? I've watched him grow up. He's like the son I never had. But, you still didn't answer my question, Orville. Why do you want to know about Doug's past?"

"Mr. Hyde has been getting threats to stop running for Congress or his past will come out."

"But, it was an accident. It wasn't Doug's fault. Just rumors. Rumors." He shook his head.

"Exactly. Rumors. That's why if it does come out, I wanted to know if you could tell the press how you examined Theresa Bigelow's body and found she wasn't pushed by Mr. Hyde or that he wasn't in shock when you treated him."

"I wish I could do that, but I was away when the accident happened."

"Away?"

"Yes, I was hunting with a few of my friends."

"Who?" I wanted to have names to verify Dr. Alden's story.

Dr. Alden seemed too weary to question me, "Bobby Kingston, Lee Stevenson, and Johnny Gagnon."

"Wasn't Kingston chief of police?" I interrupted.

"Yes, until ten years ago."

"The other names sound familiar too."

"Well, Lee Stevenson was a doctor. He just retired. And Johnny was the only dentist in Belltown for many years so you must've heard your parents mention him. We went hunting for eight days, and came back to the horrible news."

Solid alibi, I thought.

"But, Mr. Hyde thought you treated him?"

"I did but that was when I returned from my trip. He was in a sad state."

"What do you mean?"

He leaned in. "Well, the doctor who was treating him for shock was a rookie and overprescribed his medication. Doug was like a zombie for a month."

My heart was jumping again.

"Who was the doctor?"

"The same doctor who forgot to take pictures when he did the autopsy on Theresa." He stopped and took a gulp of his coffee. "I shouldn't bad-mouth someone in my profession. But I detest incompetence, and anyway he only lasted a year. He was more into the wealth from being a doctor than the wealth from helping people. He went back into his family business. It was more in his ballpark." He laughed to himself.

"What's his name?" I was eager to hear.

"Oh, sorry—Milton Hornsby."

"Milton Hornsby. The name sounds..."

"As in Hornsby Funeral Home. I just wish either Dr. Stevenson or myself didn't go on the trip to Maine. We would have had Doug under better supervision."

"Maine?" The word made me think of the clinic where Douglas Hyde was a patient.

"Yes, that's where we hunted. We stayed in a great little log cabin that..."

The intercom interrupted us, "Dr. Alden, please come to room 131. Dr. Alden, room 131."

"If you will excuse me, Orville. A patient of mine had a stroke last night. I'm afraid this could be serious."

"But," I started and realized I had to let him go.

I believed Dr. Alden had nothing to do with Theresa Bigelow's death, and I was relieved at the thought. What I wasn't relieved about was the idea of a new suspect— Milton Hornsby. Was he just a green doctor or was he a murderer? And how was he connected with Jordan Bigelow? I was sick of asking questions, but my gut told me I wouldn't have to ask too many more. There was one place that might have some answers—The Hornsby Funeral Home.

CHAPTER
NINE

THE BITING, COLD WIND sent shivers up my spine while I hid behind some bushes staking out the Hornsby Funeral Home. I really wish Gina was here with her truck, I thought as I tried to shake the cold away. I had called but only got her answering machine. I left a message for her to meet me behind the funeral home, but she still hadn't showed. I have to go solo on this mission, I thought. The question was, what was the mission? I really didn't know. Something told me that Milton Hornsby had a hand in Theresa Bigelow's death, and there would be some proof of it in his funeral home.

I rubbed my gloves together to maintain circulation and wondered if I had let that irrational voice in my head take complete control of me. After all, the accident, I mean murder happened in 1962, so why would there be evidence lying around in the funeral home? I almost convinced myself I was crazy and was about to head for home when the man I was watching through my mini-binoculars walked out of the building. I recognized him from many funerals—he was of medium build, around his mid-sixties, and wore a toupée to try to fool the world into thinking that maybe he was in his fifties. He didn't fool me! I knew immediately, it was Milton Hornsby. He went over to his car, unlocked the door, hesitated for a second, and then got in and drove off.

"It's now or never," I whispered myself into action.

I had two things going for me—the 5:30 PM hour brought the night to camouflage me, and the building looked dark. The question was, how was I going to get in? I eased down a small hill that lead to the side of the funeral home, which was connected to a two-car garage. I pulled one of the doors up just enough so I could slide under it, and as I crawled in a loud bang froze me. When I caught my breath, I realized the wind had blown the garage door down. I hopped to my feet and clicked my flashlight on to survey my surroundings. There was a truck with the Hornsby Funeral Home logo in one parking space. I guessed the truck was probably used to transport coffins. The other space was occupied by a black hearse. I shuddered for a second at the view of it and moved my light along in search of a door that lead inside.

After a couple of seconds, I found some steps and then a doorknob. I hurried up the steps and stopped in front of the door, wondering how I was going to break in. I knew the door was probably locked, but I decided to check anyway. Sometimes I got lucky. I turned the knob, and couldn't believe it—jackpot! The door opened. The adrenaline really started to kick in at this point because there was no turning back. I had broken into places before, but this time I was going on my biggest hunch. What if I was wrong? There would be no way to justify breaking the law, I thought. Shut up, I yelled in my mind. I couldn't afford to waste time going over the moral issues—I had to find proof.

I walked slowly down the hallway flashing my light low to the ground, so it wouldn't be visible from the outside. The sweet smell of flowers permeated the home, leaving an eerie feeling; even in the darkness it reminded me of the wakes I had attended. I had to find Hornsby's office. I cautiously moved on. I turned into a room that didn't have windows, so I figured I could flash my light freely around the room. I shrieked as the light shined on an old man lying in a coffin. I dropped the flashlight in cold fright. I stood inches from the body, feeling the presence beside me. I breathed deeply and picked up the light.

"Calm down," I whispered to myself as I realized the setup was for a wake. I put the flashlight on a sign by the door—"Carl Baker, Hours: Monday 10-2:00—7-9:30."

I was about to leave the room when I heard the soud of a door slamming shut. It came from the direction of the door that lead to the garage. Maybe, it's just my mind playing tricks on me, I thought, as I tried to listen for more sounds. I heard them—footsteps. I had to move quickly. I flashed my light back on the casket and spotted rows and rows of flowers beside it. It was the only place to hide as the footsteps were moving closer. I ducked behind the flowers and tried to control my breathing. I peeked through the flowers and saw the silhouette of a figure looking in. Should I try to charge right past him? My mind tried working out a plan.

"Orville," the voice whispered.

I almost knocked over the flowers at the sound of my name.

"Orville, you there?" A flashlight scanned the room. "It's me, Gina."

"Gina," I whispered, "over here."

Gina jumped, but it was not at the sound of my voice. When her light had swept the room, she had seen the old man in the coffin.

"Gina, what are you doing here?" I ran over to her.

"I came to get you."

"Get me? You mean help me."

"No, I mean get you. You're not going to find anything here. You'll never guess who I just talked to." Gina was excited.

"Who?"

"I'll tell you when we get out of here. C'mon let's hurry."

"Wait... you knocked over that man's flowers. You better pick them up." Gina put her light on the flower arrangement that was now scattered on the floor. I turned and went over to fix the arrangement when the lights went on.

"Gina, don't turn the lights on." I turned back to face her, and my eyes popped at the sight. Gina was lying motionless on the ground and there, standing above her with a gun pointed directly at me, was Milton Hornsby.

"What did you..." I tried to form words but couldn't.

"Don't worry, Orville. I just gave her a little something to make her sleep for a while."

"Sir, I'm sorry we broke into your..."

"Please, save your tired excuses. We both know why you are here. Now, pick up your friend and drag her into my office. And don't try anything stupid. Let's face it, I could tell the cops that you broke in and I feared for my life and shot you. I would easily be justified, and as a token of my own personal sadness at the event, I wouldn't even charge your parents for the funeral." He laughed, "Now, come on and hurry up."

I put my shaking hands under Gina's arms and literally dragged her down the hall and into the office. Hornsby flicked on the light and kept the gun on me.

"Take a seat," he said casually, as he sat down at his desk.

I couldn't think straight. I couldn't believe what was happening to Gina and me.

"So, how much do you know?" He folded his hands in his lap.

"Know? I ... ah ... don't ... know ... nothing..."

"I don't know anything is the correct English. Isn't your father an English teacher?" He asked.

I nodded.

"Anyway, you probably don't know much, but the fact that you're here tells me you know enough." Hornsby picked up the phone with one hand and put it to his ear. He kept one eye on me and the other one on the numbers he dialed.

"Hello, it's me." He waited a couple of seconds.

"Well, that might fool the cops but guess who I found snooping around?" he said, agitated. I was guessing that whoever was on the other line was telling Hornsby about the setup of Patrick Belavance.

"No, I can't use the crematory oven because I have a safety switch on it. I only use it early in the morning. It's too much of a risk."

The way he talked about disposing of our bodies made me sink into shock.

"Also, Gina Goldman, that friend of his, is here."

He waited and then said, "No, the ground is too frozen ... yeah, OK ... that sounds good ... Yeah, I have a couple of them in my truck."

He stared at me and listened and then said, "Hey, this whole thing is your fault. You had to bring it all up, again." He hung up.

"I can't believe that!"

"What?" I managed.

"What? Well, if you must know I knew you were going to be trouble the moment that Hyde girl went to your house."

"So, were you the one who tried to run me over with the snowplow?" Keep talking, I said to myself, I have to think of a plan.

"No, he was." He pointed to the phone.

"Who is he?"

"Don't worry, Orville, you'll get your explanation before you die."

"Die?" I gulped.

"You really don't think we're going to let you live, do you?"

"But, I don't know anything."

"You would have figured it all out soon enough. It's not the hardest equation to solve. Now get up." He waved the gun.

I stood up and faced him.

"Now, turn around."

"No," I tried to be defiant.

"Turn around or I'll shoot you right here. Right now."

I reluctantly turned around and then suddenly felt a sharp pain on the back of my head and....

I woke up and tried to focus, but it was pitch black. I was disoriented. Where was I? For some reason I felt cramped. I wondered, and then it all came back to me. What was going on?

My head was throbbing, and I guessed Hornsby must've hit me with his gun.

But, where was I now? There wasn't a light in sight, and there seemed to be no sound at all, not even the sound of the night. I had to get up and find Gina. I slowly raised my body off the floor, but my head struck something and I fell back down. It suddenly dawned on me that the floor wasn't a floor. It was soft, pillowy. Strange, I thought as I put my hands above me to feel what my head had banged. It was wooden, and it wasn't just above my head. It was above my whole body. Was it floorboards? I guessed. Then I remembered the words. They made sense now. The words Hornsby had said on the phone flowed from my mouth, "I have a couple of them in the truck." *Coffins*! I was lying in a coffin! The fear of claustrophobia gripped my entire body as I tried to push the coffin open. It didn't even budge an inch. I felt the sweat begin to break out on my forehead and soak my clothes as I pushed again and again. Trapped. Trapped like a firefly in a jelly jar with no hope of freedom. I kept pushing until my mind accepted that it was futile.

"Oh, my God! Oh, my God!" I shouted.

I was going to lie here and slowly suffocate. Why couldn't he have shot me and gotten it over with? That was too easy.

Hornsby wanted me to pay for uncovering his secrets. The worst part was I was going to die without knowing what I really uncovered. I also felt sick at the thought that my curiosity at finding the truth was going to cost Gina her life too.

"It's not fair!" I yelled and pounded my fist on the coffin. I could taste the salty tears as they rolled down the side of my face. Then, I remembered something else Hornsby had told me, "Don't worry, you'll get your explanation before you die!" I prayed silently that the madman hadn't been lying to me and that I would see the world one more time. If he was telling the truth, I knew it would be my last chance to escape, and I would need all the courage and energy possible. I took a deep breath and fought back the tears of anger and prayed softly that this coffin wasn't my eternal resting place.

CHAPTER
TEN

I PUT MY ARM IN FRONT of my face to shield my eyes from the blinding light.

"Come on, get outta there!" A voice snapped. It wasn't Hornsby's.

I rubbed my eyes, got out of the coffin, and stumbled out of the truck into the night. I sucked in the chilling Belltown breeze by the gallon while thanking God that I was still alive. But, for how much longer? The question whipped through my head like the winter wind.

"OK, walk over here," the voice commanded, and all I could make out behind the light was the man's arm waving me on. I moved closer to the man with the flashlight, but turned my head to make out where we were. It didn't take me long to figure out the location. It seemed like years, but I had been there only the night before— Pilgrim Pond.

"Hornsby, you got the girl?" the man shouted.

"Yeah, but she's still out cold."

"That's OK. Drag her over here by her boyfriend."

"Who are you and what's this all about?" I asked angrily.

"Hey, keep your voice down, kid." He put the gun in front of the flashlight so I could see it. I don't know anything about guns, but I knew enough to know that it resembled the same gun Hornsby had hit me with. I thought, keep a mental note of that—perhaps, one gun, two of them.

"I'm sorry, sir. I'm scared." Obviously, I was, but by saying it, I thought he might think that I wasn't a threat.

"Well, you should be scared. You're finally going to learn your lesson about what happens when you look into other people's business. I have to give you credit, though, Hornsby warned me about you, but I said he's just a kid. That is, until you made it out of the harbor alive." Hornsby then appeared dragging Gina and dumped her unconscious body next to me.

"I told Orville you would give him an explanation." Hornsby walked over to the man.

"An explanation—is that what you want?" The man asked.

"You're Jordan Bigelow, aren't you?" I took a stab in the dark. Both of them began laughing.

"You think *I'm* Jordan Bigelow?"

"Yes, you killed your daughter for the insurance money. You probably pushed your wife off the Belltown Heights Hill and cashed in her policy, too."

"I think we overestimated you, Orville," said Hornsby.

"No, he's got some of the pieces right, but I'm certainly not that fool Bigelow."

"Then who are you.

"My name is Willard Shelton."

"Willard Shelton?" I snapped my fingers. "You were Bigelow's lawyer."

"Bravo. You *are* worthy of dying after all." Shelton flicked off his flashlight so I could see his face. I was expecting to see the fierce face of a killer, but he was as nondescript looking as Hornsby, except he didn't wear a toupée. He was bald and in his sixties.

"I don't get it. Any of it."

"Well, what do you think, Hornsby? Should I tell him?"

"Why not, I've always wanted to tell someone to see their reaction. It's such a fascinating tale."

"OK, Orville. I guess we'll start on June 15, 1961."

"But, Theresa died on May 4, 1962."

They both laughed and Hornsby said, "You're telling us."

"On June 15, 1961, Theresa's mother, Joanne Bigelow, took a walk on an extremely foggy night and died from a fall off the Belltown Heights Hill. Jordan Bigelow came to me and begged me to give him an alibi because he was also taking a walk that night, and a week earlier he had purchased an insurance policy on her life."

"So, he killed his wife?"

"No, I did. That's the beauty of it. By giving him an

alibi he was giving me one. So I told the police Jordan and I had been playing cards all night."

"Why did you kill her?"

"I loved Joanne. She was the only person I have ever loved ... Well, anyway, I set up the life insurance policies for the whole family."

"Three hundred thousand a piece," I said.

"Very good work. Except Jordan's was for four hundred thousand. Anyway, I told Joanne that night how I felt about her and said that I would kill Jordan and she would get the money and we would be together forever. She said she'd never leave him. She thought I was crazy."

She was right on target, I thought. He was so calm, like he was telling a bedtime story and not a recounting of his madness.

"I lost control when she told me her feelings and pushed her off the hill, and she fell fifty feet to her death. If I couldn't have her for my wife, neither could Jordan Bigelow. I wanted to have something over Jordan, so I gave him an alibi for that night. Even as he grieved, he knew it looked odd that he had just bought the policy and a week later his wife was dead." Shelton stopped and turned to Hornsby, "Why don't you take care of you know what."

"Just when it was getting to my part." Hornsby shook his head and walked over to the truck and got something out of it. I guessed it was antifreeze. They probably intended to force Gina and me onto the ice so we would fall through like Vanessa. I had to keep Shelton talking, but it didn't seem to be a problem. He seemed to enjoy his story.

"Do you mind?" he asked as he pulled out a flask.

"No, not at all." I was trying to be just as calm and unemotional.

"Hornsby thinks I drink too much. Well, where was I?"

"You told me how you killed Joanne Bigelow, but you didn't explain why you killed Theresa."

"Oh, yes. Well, you see in exchange for the alibi that I had given Jordan Bigelow, he made me a silent partner in his clothing business. But, I wanted it all. So, I got to thinking what is the one thing that would make Jordan Bigelow give up the business—his daughter. Theresa was the only person who kept him living." He took a hard swallow from the flask but kept the gun and his eyes on me.

"Yeah, but how did you know that after Theresa died Jordan Bigelow wouldn't just put all his time and energy into the business instead of selling it to you?

"You ask a lot of questions. But, you're right. That was what I didn't know. So, one night I was talking to Hornsby, who is also my best friend, and we figured out a foolproof plan that would not only get me the business but also get us both some serious money. We watched Theresa for weeks to learn her patterns, and we found out that she and Doug Hyde liked to play by the train tracks. So, one night when we were watching them, we heard Theresa say that her birthday was coming and she wanted Doug to help her sneak away from the party and go to the railroad tracks. I knew that would be the best night to work our plan." He took another healthy swig. I knew with each swallow my chances of escaping got better. Once the alcohol kicked in, he would let down his guard. At least, that is what I was hoping.

"Dr. Alden, Stevenson, Gagnon, and Bobby Kingston, who was chief of police, were avid hunters and I told them that they could use my log cabin for eight days. But, they had to use it immediately because I was going to rent it out for the summer. They all pulled some strings to get the time off, and Hornsby and I were lucky they did."

"What does that have..."

"If you want to hear the story stop interrupting or I can just throw you in the pond now!" The alcohol was getting to him. He took another swig and calmed down a bit. "Hornsby and I were waiting in the woods for Theresa and Doug. And, like clockwork, they arrived ten minutes before the next train. Hornsby put some drugs on two rags and I took care of Doug and he took care of Theresa and then..." He stopped and looked over at Gina who was coming to. "Ah, darn, I was just getting to the punch line." Shelton shook his head.

"This still doesn't make sense. Why did you black-mail Doug Hyde?" I tried to keep him interested in the story.

"I didn't even finish Theresa's role in all of it, the Doug Hyde part is years later but I'm afraid we don't have time."

"Orville ... what happened ... oh, my head." Gina staggered to her feet, and then she saw the gun pointed at us. "Oh, my God!"

"Keep it down, little girl," Shelton warned.

Hornsby then appeared out of the darkness.

"She's awake, huh?"

"Yeah, she just woke up."

"You tell the kid?" Hornsby asked.

"Up until the good part, but we can't stick around any longer. How's the ice?"

"Ready to go." Hornsby threw two empty jugs into the back of the truck.

"OK, come on you two. We're going to take a little walk." Shelton waved the gun toward the pond.

"Orville, are they going to..." Gina looked at me.

"Shut up and keep walking," Shelton snapped.

"If we run, what are you going to do? Shoot both of us with one gun?" I asked. I had to find out if Hornsby was carrying a gun or if the gun Shelton was holding was Hornsby's.

"That's a stupid question. All I need is two bullets. And Hornsby, you loaded two bullets, didn't you?"

"A full barrel."

Gina got my point—one gun. She gave me a look before she turned to Shelton. "I don't want to die." She sobbed into her hands.

I knew exactly what she was doing.

"Shut up." Shelton moved toward her.

"I don't want to die." She sobbed again.

"Come on. I said shut up." Shelton moved within a foot of Gina.

In a lightning quick action, Gina karate-chopped his

hand and he dropped the gun. Everyone dove for the gun. I punched and kicked Hornsby and crawled toward the gun lying in the snow. I reached out and almost grabbed it when Gina accidentally kicked it out of my reach as she struggled with Shelton. Hornsby kicked me in the head, bounced to his feet, and sprinted for the gun when a distant sound of a siren paralyzed him just enough for me to gain my balance and jump him. We tumbled and wrestled on the ground and I grabbed anything I could to get leverage. Suddenly, I heard, "Don't move or I'll shoot!"

I looked up and Gina had the gun.

I sighed in relief and then realized I was holding Hornsby's toupée. Any other time I would have laughed, but I just threw it in the direction of the pond and went over to Gina. Shelton and Hornsby lay on the ground moaning in disbelief.

Blue and white lights then colored the winter sky and Officer Jameson leaped out of his cruiser.

"What the..." He looked at the scene.

Gina walked over and handed him the gun. "You can take care of them, Officer Jameson."

"What are you talking about, Gina? A neighbor called and said she saw someone on Pilgrim Pond's ice. She thought it might not be safe." Officer Jameson had no clue as to what he had stumbled onto.

"Cuff them and we'll explain all of it down at the station."

"On what grounds, Orville?"

"How about they just tried to kill Gina and me. But

if you want something bigger, how about for the murders of Joanne Bigelow and Theresa Bigelow."

"I didn't kill Joanne Bigelow. And I certainly didn't kill Theresa Bigelow," Milton Hornsby shouted.

"We'll settle this down at the station." Officer Jameson went over and cuffed Hornsby first. Willard Shelton was still lying on the ground in pain. Gina had done quite a job on him. Jameson barked for back up into his radio.

"He's telling the truth about Theresa Bigelow." Gina turned to me, "Orville, they didn't kill her."

"What do you mean they didn't kill her?" I asked in amazement.

"Because I talked to her before I went to the funeral home."

"What, are you crazy?"

Gina looked directly into my eyes, "Orville, that's what I was trying to tell you at Hornsby's. Theresa Bigelow is alive."

Back at the police station, it took about four cups of coffee before the puzzle was finally put together.

"This is the most unbelievable story ever." Shane poured another cup.

"I know I heard it from Hornsby. He's going to testify against Willard Shelton. He's going to plea bargain."

"Yeah, so much for best friends," I muttered.

"I still don't believe it. Are you guys ready to hear it?"

"Of course, we almost died because of it," Gina said.

"OK, try not to interrupt because I want to keep all the facts straight," Shane kidded us.

"Shane!" Gina and I both said.

"OK, Milton Hornsby was straight out of med school in 1962. It was his first year out when Willard Shelton put his plan to work. Shelton made sure that Belltown's other two doctors were out of town plus the dentist and the chief of police. So, while they were hunting up in the woods of Maine, Milton Hornsby took a body from his father's funeral home; a body that he said he was supposed to cremate. A small woman, a car accident victim."

"How sick!" Gina blurted.

"I know. Anyway, the body was already in bad shape They put a dress on the body, put it on the tracks, and kidnapped Theresa Bigelow. Since Milton Hornsby was the only doctor in town at the time, he examined the body. The dentist was hunting too, so there were no dental records to be checked. And it was considered an accident anyway. Also, the chief of police was with the group of hunters so the cop in charge handled the investigation. They say he never had experienced an accident scene and, like most first time cops, his stomach turned at the sight and he went by everything Dr. Hornsby reported. Hornsby also told the officer that he would take the body to the funeral home at the wishes of Jordan Bigelow who wanted his daughter cremated."

"So, he was able to return the body and no one noticed it missing," I said. I couldn't believe what I was hearing.

"Exactly. Two weeks later, Shelton and Hornsby notified Jordan Bigelow that his daughter was alive. They told him to bring them the three hundred thousand dollars of insurance money as a ransom and as blackmail. Bigelow had no idea how they pulled it off, but, since his wife had died so mysteriously, he didn't think anyone would ever believe he didn't have anything to do with it. He thought he had no choice but to give them the money."

"I don't know, I'd still go to the police," Gina said.

"Jordan Bigelow probably thought the police were involved too. After all, a body had been found and police were at the scene. You would naturally think they were the ones covering it up," Shane said.

"Good point." I nodded for him to continue.

"Shelton warned Bigelow never to come back to Cape Cod or he would have his daughter killed. So, Bigelow moves out of town. Doesn't tell anyone where he's going but sends one letter back to Belltown out of guilt for blaming a little boy for his daughter's death."

"But why blackmail Doug Hyde years later?" Gina asked the question that had driven me crazy for days.

"It's all about fish. Willard Shelton owns Shelton's Shellfish and Seafood Company. He owns a whole fleet of boats that fish in Fisherman's Banks." Shane took a sip of his coffee.

"I knew this had something to do with Fisherman's Banks." I pumped my fist.

"Yeah, if Hyde is elected and the bill he's proposing passes, Shelton would have been ruined. Hornsby said that got the idea to blackmail Hyde when he was hunting up in Maine with a buddy who worked in a mental hospital."

"Oh, man, what a coincidence." I shook my head.

"Yeah, the friend told Shelton that Hyde had been a patient and all he talked about was his friend getting hit by a train, and his daughter drowning. Shelton being the sicko that he is had saved some of the things from the kidnapping like a piece of the dress and a flattened penny. He figured if he sent a couple of letters, it would drive Hyde crazy and he'd drop out of the race. He didn't figure on Orville Jacques." Shane smiled.

"And Gina Goldman," I added.

"Yeah, I hear you gave Shelton quite a karate chop."

"You can thank my sensei for teaching me that. Wipe on. Wipe off." We all laughed for a minute.

"What I don't get is the tip you got about the death threat on Orville? And also Patrick Belavance and all the evidence on his boat?" Gina asked.

Shane nodded. "Once they realized Orville was snooping around, they decided to take care of him and shift the blame on someone else. They phoned it in. As for the fisherman, Patrick Belavance, Shelton heard what Belavance had said about Hyde and figured he was perfect to set up. I do owe that guy an apology." Shane nodded in thought.

"But, my questions are what was Theresa Bigelow's reaction when you talked to her, and how did you find her, Gina?"

"I was looking for her father's name and found hers.

She was the only Bigelow in Case City. My eyes popped out of my head when I saw her name, and I decided to call. To make a long story short, we were both in shock. She said she always had a dream, and she suspected something but her father insisted it was a dream. He never told her about Belltown. He said they had lived in San Diego when she was little and..." Gina didn't finish her sentence because Mr. Hyde walked into the room. He had been in the other office talking to Theresa on the phone. The room was silent in anticipation. Mr. Hyde's eyes were filled with tears as he came over and hugged both Gina and me and said, "Thank you. Thank you for giving back my Theresa."

I simply said, "You're welcome." After all, I was just doing my job.

My clock radio went off at 6:45 AM. I groaned and hit the snooze alarm and thought about everything that had happened. By far, it had been my craziest case but also it had been the happiest ending. Mr. Hyde and Theresa Bigelow had planned a reunion. Mr. Hyde said Theresa told him she had never married because she felt empty as though there were someone missing in her life, but she never could find him. She would find herself looking for him in movie theaters, parks, and crowded malls, but never found him. I'm not Cupid, but if fate had its way, who knew what the reunion would lead to? The snooze alarm went off again and the DJ brought me back to the moment.

"Oh, no, it's Monday. I have to make up that test for Mr. Reasons," I moaned and forced myself out of bed. I went to open the drapes when the DJ said, "We're looking at twelve to fifteen inches of snow out there! On a day like this I don't even have to read the school cancellations. Everything's canceled."

"It's a joke. It has to be," I said, and pulled open my drapes and was greeted by a glorious white landscape. *Snow day*—the greatest combination of two words known to man.

"No test! Not today, Mr. Reasons!" I laughed out of control.

Psyched. On top of the world. That's how I felt. The phone rang and I picked it up.

"Hi, Orville. It's Vanessa."

"Oh, hi, Vanessa. What's up?" My heart skipped a beat.

"I just wanted to thank you for everything you did. I mean, I can't even begin to thank you, really."

"No problem! How are you feeling?"

"Oh, fine. I wasn't even going to miss school today, but thank goodness for the snow… I'm …that was the other reason I was calling. I know it's really early, but I was wondering if you would want to get some breakfast and maybe go sledding or something?"

"Yeah, that sounds like fun," I said with a full smile on my face. Psyched. On top of the world. Yup, that's exactly how I felt!

About the Author

T. M. Murphy lives in Falmouth, Massachusetts. When he is not writing or cheering for the Boston Red Sox, Mr. Murphy enjoys teaching creative writing to young people. He lives and teaches his Just Write It class in a converted garage he calls The Shack.

Check out www.belltownmysteries.com and www.jntownsendpublishing.com.